The Passion of Marta

A NOVEL

CAREN UMBARGER

THE PASSION OF MARTA

ISBN-13: 978-1977936196
ISBN-10: 1977936199

LCCN: 2017915501

CreateSpace Independent Publishing Platform
North Charleston, South Carolina

for the children

The violin – that most human of all instruments

~ LOUISA MAY ALCOTT

Where words fail, music speaks

~ HANS CHRISTIAN ANDERSON

The Passion of Marta

Prologue

Part I

Wherein a lady's violin is made
in Nuremberg, Germany 1782

Part II

Ascher's Remembrance
Jebenhausen, Germany 1782

Part III

Marta's Diary
Jebenhausen, Germany 1789

Prologue

A chilling wind whips against the queue waiting to board ship. All along the wharf, families huddle together for warmth. Men turn away to shield their faces from the icy blasts, and women tighten their headscarves, pull their children close and blink their watering eyes against the biting October cold.

Each clutches an invisible ember of hope deep within, like a charm to ward off peril. A new and better life waits across the water – seven, eight, or maybe a dozen weeks and countless unknown dangers, hardships and miseries from where they now stand.

As the line slowly makes its way up the gangplank and onto the ship, a young couple struggles to wend their way through the old town and down to the water's edge in time to board the last embarkation of the season. Their stooped shoulders and worn, dirty clothes distinguish them as peasants who have already traveled far, like most of those making the journey.

A heavy bundle on his back and the cold north wind in his face hinder the man's progress. His skin is sallow, his mouth is set in a grim line. He is thin as a stalk, his legs are spent and buckle outwards every few steps.

The woman is smaller. She leans into the bluster with determined resolve. Her skirts are smudged and torn, and her blue flapping shawl is wrapped around her head and face so that only her squinted eyes feel the raw sting of the late season gusts. Her pack is lopsided, askew.

After their arduous journey they say little; a grunt here, a nod there. Their plan is almost complete – the ship is within sight. It is all they can do to propel themselves forward toward their unknown, uncertain future.

At the quay they join the few left in line. They remain bent under their heavy loads and slowly move up the gangplank toward the ship's deck. At the top, the man pulls a small purse from his pocket, finds the money he has preserved, and pays their way on board. They will not be indentured when they arrive in America. They will be free. But, they will disembark in the New World with little more than what they carry with them.

At the ladder to the hold, the man hands his pack along to waiting arms below, then eases himself down into the dark chaos that will be their home for the duration. He reaches up to receive the bundle she has removed with care from her back. It is a wooden case wrapped in leather and tied with rope - a precious violin swaddled securely within.

Gently, with tears of happiness, she eases her package into the hands of her beloved husband and watches as it disappears into the hold.

The woman turns to back down the steps with careful attention for she, too, carries a priceless cargo - the tiny growing child who will awaken along with them to the light of the New World.

Part I

CHAPTER 1

Leopold Wilhelm, violinmaker
Nuremberg, Germany
February, 1782

The church bell in the center of town toned deeply five times, and on the sixth, the young luthier stretched luxuriantly beneath the quilt, opened his eyes, and squinted against the morning light that streamed through the small window beside the bed. Vague remnants of his dream faded… *was there a ship?* … and then disappeared forever.

He rolled over, stretched again, then lay still and turned his attention to his wife as she stood with her back to him at the window. She looked high out over the walls of the city and pulled the brush through her long hair.

Down below in the street, she watched as the Hauptmarkt vendors set out their wares for the day in front of the old Frauenkirche, a church that had endured for centuries, as had the market square.

The vegetable man unhitched his horse from its cart and led it to a grassy area behind, then returned to straighten up his offerings; a few papery onions, some knobby old carrots, a pile of parsnips, turnips, and potatoes. He had several bunches of watercress, but that was all. It was too early for any other greens.

Next to him, Üte watched old stooped Hilde, the soap monger, remove the leather harness from around her own chest, lay it gently on the ground and wedge a broken brick to stabilize the two-wheeled cart she hauled around the town like an ox. Her rough bars of soap were harsh on Üte's hands, but often it was all they could afford. It had been many months since Leopold had sold a violin.

A spotted dog sniffed around in front of the butcher's door where another vendor sat hunched over a stone on his low stool, sharpening his knife. Üte thought of Leopold in his workshop, of the many hours he spent bent over his stone as he honed his knives, his chisels and the blades for his planes. And then, how many more hours he sawed, and took wood away with the chisel and plane – rubbed fine sand over and over with the grain until the graduations and gentle curves became smooth as river stones.

It was painstaking work. Already, at twenty-seven he walked with a stoop despite her efforts to remind him to stand up straight. She bent forward, threw her hair over in front of her and brushed down hard.

On this particular morning, early spring sunshine danced through her thin muslin gown against the light from the window. Leopold, still silent and motionless in his bed, repeatedly traced the clear glowing outline of her body beneath the cloth with his eyes. *How female the violin form is. Is it any wonder that I can't wait to get to work in the mornings?*

Üte was newly recovered from the influenza that had nearly taken her during the winter. She was gaunt and pale and carried not an extra gram anywhere on her small frame. Her pelvic bones showed clearly through the cloth, their sharp outline intensified by the startling indentation of her waistline. The muscles of her backside had atrophied as she had lain for weeks in her bed so that now he saw the actual shape of her bone and muscle structure rather than the soft curves and plump, rounded contours he remembered.

To Leopold, her new conformation was a revelation. As he visually traced and re-traced her image, an ecstatic wave blossomed through him. This was it! In his mind he committed the forms he saw beneath the gauzy cloth to memory. He imagined drawing them on paper – saw himself draw the movement of the lines and shapes of the curves until, when he finally looked away, the outline of her monumental classical form was indelibly etched in his consciousness.

For months he had searched for a creative idea – some way to bring forth a new violin with a unique shape that would set him apart from Stainer and Klotz and the others whose instruments were always asked after in his shop. He was particularly interested in producing a violin that would outshine all of the instruments made by his father and brother in their violin shop in Vienna.

Leopold and Üte had moved from Vienna to Nuremberg to set up their own shop three years before, and ever since then, Leopold had harbored the friendly desire to outdo both of them at the Bavarian Luthier Guild Meeting to be held in Vienna in the Spring of 1784, two years hence.

He wanted to create a violin that would maintain the popular highly arched style but would also project more power and richness of sound, the way a Stradavarius or a Guarnari Del Gesu did. He had seen a Stradivarius once – four of them, actually.

When Leopold was fourteen years old, his father had received, in his Viennese shop, a quartet of string instruments made by Stradivari which needed to be reviewed and adjusted. Leopold, his brother and father all leapt at the opportunity to familiarize themselves with the details of craftsmanship by the most outstanding Cremonese luthier: the flatter arching with rounder curves, much like Amati's – more graceful than any of them had ever seen before – with corners like the pursed lips of angels, and carved f-holes displaying the maker's own signature style.

When he beheld those instruments, not only was his soul awakened to a beauty that, until then, he had only dreamed of in a violin, but Leopold had vowed to himself on the spot that he would carve a violin that could sing like a bird, emote like a woman and have the most pleasing physical attributes that he or anyone else had ever seen. It would be even more beautiful than the Stradivarius.

This goal was not completely out of the question for Leopold because he was slowly gaining renown as a reputable luthier whose instruments were well made and sought after in his own city of Nuremberg, and also in the surrounding towns and villages. Although sales had been slow, quite slow, during the past winter, he was determined to see his plan through.

Until this moment, when the morning's light illuminated his wife's form so vividly, Leopold had been thirsting for inspiration like a man lost in the desert. This revelation, brought to him via the sunlight and his wife's slender body, was a gift and he couldn't wait to get started on his new design.

He would have to build a mold in the new shape, Üte's shape, with that particular angularity that so appealed to him in a violin: a perfect blend of smooth curves yet visibly squared shoulders. The more he looked at her, the more excited he became.

He rolled out of bed and dressed quickly, threw water on his face and swished some around in his mouth. After he stepped to the window, he nuzzled Üte's neck. He had to get his idea down on paper.

"Üte, bring me my breakfast in the shop, please."

She looked up from her brushing to discern his mood. He looked animated and happy.

"Yes, Leopold… as soon as I get dressed. I'll have it for you right away."

He circled her waist with his large hands, kissed her, and then left her in the garret bedroom.

On the way down the narrow winding stairs, he ran both hands along the walls for balance. He passed through the kitchen at the back of the house on his way to the privy, and after, opened the cellar door and went down the steps.

On one side of the dim room were three large shelves stacked with quarter sawn and flat slabs of wood in different stages of curing: fine-grained spruce for the tops and fancy maple with striations for the backs. Leopold spent several minutes rummaging through them.

He picked up larger pieces, held them to his ear and rapped his knuckles against them. He listened for the tone that the wood released, and twice he stepped outside to see the wood's grain in the daylight. When he was satisfied that he had chosen the best possible pieces for the top, bottom, ribs and scroll of his new creation, he went back up to the house and returned through to the front of the building, to the little room that housed his shop.

Next to the forest, this was Leopold's favorite place. It was small, just one room... one tiny room. But, in this place his imagination was free to soar. Before he opened the shutters to let in the morning light, he looked around at his treasured workshop.

Above the pine bench he had fashioned, his tools hung neatly in their places on the wall. Opposite the window, five violins in different states of repair hung in a row, each on its own wire attached to a small peg. A cello top and separate body stood in the corner, and on the bottom of his four shelves sat the small brazier he used for making glue and varnish. A violin in pieces lay next to it.

He loved the smells that greeted him each morning: shaved wood, glue, and the ingredients of varnish – the earthy oils and fragrant spirits, the resins and dyes.

Even now there were thin curls of wood and fresh wood chips scattered on the floor beneath his stool. Üte never cleaned this room unless he asked her to. His normal fastidiousness suffered when he was engrossed in making, but he delighted in the mess.

He opened the shutters beside his workbench and hung the chisel he had used the day before on its peg. He had been graduating the top of a small instrument, a child's violin that the Kapellmeister at the church had commissioned for his son.

After he laid the unfinished instrument on a shelf, he swept the bench with a soft brush, pulled a large sheet of paper off a sheaf he kept loosely rolled on one of the shelves and spread it before him. Then, he chose a charcoal from the box and began to draw. Images – of Üte, of violins, of musicians – danced through his mind as he settled down to his work.

Üte knew to knock gently before she entered Leopold's shop so she waited and listened, and when she heard a pause in the soft scrapes of his drawing, she tapped her knuckles on the door. She heard him moan and a moment later he opened the door himself. His eyes burned into hers. Üte drew back and waited, but he didn't speak.

"Leopold, are you alright? Are you ill?" She steadied the tray she held in her hands. "Leopold?"

Leopold started, and then quickly shook his head.

"I'm fine, fine, Üte. Come see what I have been doing."

Üte set the tray on a corner of the bench and peered over his shoulder at the drawing. She gasped.

"It looks like a tender and strong woman at the same time! This is fine work, my husband. It's a new idea… a new shape, isn't it?" She looked at him again, and again was surprised by the intensity she saw in his face.

Leopold studied the drawing as though it was a live thing writhing before him. His head tipped to the side and in the morning light, Üte thought he looked absolutely beatific, like the saints in the frescos at church.

She glanced at the image of the violin on the paper, which pleased her, but her gaze returned to her husband's face. She had never seen him like this.

"It's beautiful, Leopold. Is it for anyone in particular?"

He hesitated before he answered. "It should be smaller, I think – small and light and easy to play, but with a big sound. I want to make the neck a bit thinner, too..."

"You're making an instrument for a small person but not a child? Is it a lady's violin?"

Leopold's eyebrows shot up.

"You know… I think you may be right. But, I'll sell it to anyone, man or woman, who'll put the right amount for it into my hands."

Üte smiled at him.

"I agree."

They stood for long moments and studied the sketch together. Then, they hugged. Maybe this was the beginning of Leopold's greatest work so far, she thought.

CHAPTER 2

One week later, Üte dried her hands on her apron as she hurried to answer the door. Leopold had mentioned earlier that the Kapellmeister's appointment was arranged for ten o'clock and the man was punctual.

"Good day, Herr Kapellmeister. Please come in. Leopold will see you now."

He bowed formally to her then followed Üte down the hall and around the corner to the door of Leopold's shop. Üte listened within before she knocked softly.

"Leopold? It's Herr Kapellmeister. He's here for

his appointment."

She surveyed the man as they stood and waited. He was middle-aged, not tall, but held himself erect. After all, he held a position of stature in the city. He was smartly dressed in vest and waistcoat of first-rate dark wool, both stretched in front to their limit as though he harbored a large gourd or pumpkin beneath, a flouncy jabot at his neck and wrists, and a queue of thinning grey hair tied back with a navy ribbon.

Although he presented as a fine fellow, his color did not look good to Üte. He was pasty white with tinges of yellowish green around his mouth and eyes, and a thin sheen of glistening sweat on his forehead. She noticed a slight tremor in his hand as he nervously fingered his timepiece. Üte searched for something to say to try to calm him.

"I hope you are enjoying this mild day, sir."

He turned his watery red-rimmed eyes toward her but before he could speak, Leopold opened the door and ushered the man into his room. Üte met Leopold's eyes briefly with a look of concern. She knew that Kapellmeister Johannes Krieger was a kind and generous man whose position as music director at St. Sebaldus Church helped maintain a continuous flow of musicians into Leopold's shop.

Krieger worked closely with Wilhelm Pachelbel, the

organist at the church, and it was common knowledge that together they produced some of the most highly respected musical offerings in the city. As one of two luthiers serving Nuremberg directly, Leopold was fortunate to be in the good graces of Krieger, and Üte hoped that the man's health would hold out. It took time to establish a respectable working relationship with musicians. Time, and an honorable man such as Krieger to act as intercessor.

As Üte closed the door, she heard the Kapellmeister clap Leopold on his back. At least he still had some vitality left in him.

The men shook hands and exchanged greetings. Leopold assumed Üte's concern had been about Krieger's obvious ill health, but he ignored that and drew him to his bench.

"Listen, Johannes, I have been remiss in finishing your son's violin." Krieger raised his eyebrows. "But, I have a good reason. Look here..."

The luthier gently lifted a white, newly graduated violin top and held it up like a newborn in the light from the window. The purfling, of which Leopold was extremely proud, had been inlaid all the way around the entire top edge. It was perfect - not one wrong gouge or stray fleck of wood.

"I'm ready to carve the f-holes. I'm planning to begin work this afternoon."

He glanced at the Kapellmeister to see his reaction. The man pursed his lips and reached tentatively for the unfinished top, so Leopold set it gently into his trembling hands. Herr Krieger checked the heft, tapped the beautiful, straight-grained spruce and listened carefully. He tipped it toward the window and peered in closely at the inlay then cleared his throat.

"Well, well, Wilhelm. It looks as though you have something here, something, indeed." When he looked at the luthier, they smiled knowingly at each other. "This is an unusual form, is it not? And, I dare say that this violin is a bit smaller and more delicate than usual, am I not correct? Is not the arching particularly high and fine - much like the best of Stainer?"

Leopold grinned like a naughty boy. For the Kapellmeister to recognize his work this way, well… he could barely contain his pleasure.

"So, you like it? Is that what you're saying?"

Krieger's response was a ferocious sneeze directly onto the violin top, then a hearty laugh that turned into a harsh, phlegmy cough. Leopold quickly snatched the precious piece away from him.

The Kapellmeister pulled a handkerchief from his pocket, held it to his mouth and coughed until he nearly choked before he finally hawked a large glob into it. Then he stuffed the cloth back into his pocket with shaking hands. Leopold guided him to his stool where he sat until he had resumed a more stable disposition. Krieger cleared his voice before he spoke.

"Wilhelm, I can see why you have not been working on the violin for my son. This lovely distraction demands all of your attention. Any of your other projects are secondary to this – am I not correct?"

Leopold looked toward the floor. He had told the Kapellmeister that he would have the boy's violin finished before the end of February, but it was now early March and he still had at least a month's work left to do on it. He had put all other tasks aside in order to indulge his own creative desire.

"Yes, you're correct, Herr Kapellmeister. I am, indeed, behind in my work because of this violin." He regarded Krieger with contrition but the man did not seem angry or even upset. He appeared pensive.

"Would it help if you could get a down payment for this new violin?"

Leopold nodded eagerly.

"Perhaps if I can help establish a suitable buyer for this instrument you will have incentive to finish mine, Wilhelm. It's not every day that a creation such as this violin of yours comes into the world, but I am impatient for my son to play on his own instrument."

A loud sneeze escaped the Kapellmeister and a potent wet breeze flew directly onto Leopold's face and chest. He used his kerchief to wipe himself off, and when Krieger regained his equilibrium, the man continued.

"Recently I traveled to Berlin and there I heard a wondrous performance of a Bach concerto by an up and coming performer. The man's name escapes me… Meinel or Mandel or something like that. And," he leaned conspiratorially toward the luthier and held his hand around his mouth with a hushed gesture, "unfortunately he is a Jew - with a somewhat shady reputation."

He waggled his eyebrows then sat up straight. "But, my what a talent. And, I tell you this because the instrument he used did not impress me… not at all. A man with that caliber of expertise should have a better instrument, even if he is a Jew. That might be a worthwhile avenue."

Leopold interjected quickly.

"Well, the man's dubious penchants interest me not. What I need to know is: does he have any money? Does he have a sponsor? It would please me to have my violin heard and seen in Berlin."

Krieger held out a hand to calm the luthier's excitement.

"I will certainly make inquiries, my friend. I have an acquaintance, the Kapellmeister of Döbbelin's theatrical troupe there, Johan Frischmuth, who may know. I would not be surprised to learn that there is money behind this man." He jotted an address on a piece of paper with the ink and quill pen from Leopold's workbench.

"I also have news that two composers will be traveling through Nuremberg and are scheduled to perform later this spring; one of the Bach brothers, Johann Christian, and also Wolfgang Mozart. He is a marvel on the violin and may be interested in seeing this one of yours. Perhaps I can send an encouraging letter to them regarding what you are bringing forth. Let me think about these ideas and see what I can come up with. I will plan to get back to you with thoughts about a buyer within a fortnight and by then you will have made considerable progress on my son's violin, yes?"

In a fortnight Leopold could carve the scroll, the f-holes, shape the fingerboard and pegs, and glue the top, sides and back of the small violin together. But, he would not have time to hang it in the white and let the sun promote its rich shading before he painted layers of oil varnish into its fine grain.

More importantly, if he were to spend as much time on the child's instrument as he knew he should, it would leave him no time to work on the violin he loved most, the one he thought of as Üte's violin.

"I will do my best, Herr Kapellmeister, to finish the

little violin for the lad." But, as he spoke, he wondered just how he was going to accomplish all that needed doing before two weeks was up. He had never before felt such pressure. Violin making was normally a slow, careful process; it was not to be hurried.

Johannes Krieger coughed violently into his handkerchief. When he was finished, he turned toward Leopold. With his rheumy eyes and red nose he resembled Abbo, the town idiot. But, Leopold understood the lofty musical talent and kind heart that resided in that rotund body. Again, the Kapellmeister cleared his throat.

"Thank you, Herr Luthier, you do excellent work. I trust that you will follow through on our plan." He reached his hand toward Leopold, who shook it with a firm clasp and an affirmative nod.

As he escorted the Kapellmeister to the door, Leopold's thoughts churned. He hadn't known such joy could be his simply from making a beautiful instrument. It would be a trial to pull himself from the work he loved in order to finish a violin that he now cared little for. In actuality, he cared little for anything in life, save Üte and the violin he labored over day after day.

CHAPTER 3

Üte pulled the hood of her cape further over her brow and leaned against Leopold as they half-ran and stumbled through the rain. Leopold hunched deeper in his hat and coat under the downpour but did not escape it. By the time they reached home, his clothing was sodden and he shivered from the chilly dampness.

"Here, Leopold, get out of these wet clothes - I'll put the kettle on."

She hung her cape on a peg then walked back to the kitchen, but Leopold stood inside the door, dumbfounded. He still could not believe that Johannes

Krieger was dead – it was his funeral they had just attended. It had not been three weeks since the man's visit to the shop, barely three weeks since the two had shaken hands over the future of his violins in progress.

It was bad news enough to lose Krieger; the man had helped secure a steady stream of instrumentalists through Leopold's door. And, Leopold liked him – his ready laugh and high standards. Few men strove for and actually achieved such consistently excellent musical programs.

Now he was going to be hard pressed to receive payment for the child's violin because the man was a widower. With no wife to preside over his finances, the estate could be tied up indefinitely, and the child's custodian would surely guard any monies, especially those for purchases considered frivolous or extravagant. Krieger had mentioned that the small violin for his son was probably not a necessary purchase but rather an indulgence, and the two men had enjoyed the prospect of an unexpected gift for the boy.

When Üte returned to the hallway she found Leopold where she had left him, lost in thought.

"Husband, come in now and dry off. You'll be sick yourself if we're not careful."

She helped him settle into a chair at the table, wrapped a blanket around his shoulders, and then served him a cup of tea.

"Üte, I believe I will set aside the lad's violin for the time being."

She sat down across from him. Rain fell so hard that they had to raise their voices to be heard over the noise.

"I cannot be sure that I would be paid for it, even if I were to finish it. Krieger mentioned that the purchase for his boy was an extravagance. I think I will wait to hear whether the family wants it or not. And, the truth is, I am compelled by a strong desire to finish this new one."

As he set his teacup back into the saucer, a chill sent a hard shiver through his body which made the cup clatter and spill. Üte reached out to steady his hand, and then she stretched up and felt his forehead.

"If that is a fever I feel coming on, Leopold, you must go directly to your bed. We have seen seven poor souls in town pass away in these last weeks... I don't want you to join them!"

"But the violin, Üte... I must finish this violin. I must..."

"What difference is a violin if you are lost to the influenza? And what shall I do without you if you go, too?" She covered her mouth with her napkin as her eyes filled with tears.

Leopold did not mention the slight headache and

sore throat that had plagued him all morning. It was imperative that he finish her violin immediately. If he became too ill - or worse - then she could sell it and have some means with which to support herself for a time.

The young luthier looked across the table at his devoted wife, so thin and sickly herself, and fought the idea that either one of them might not survive this latest outbreak of influenza. There was talk of epidemic, and from what he had witnessed in town it was probably true. He sought to calm her fears.

"Üte, my darling, I'm fine. I will finish this violin as swiftly as I can - there's little left to do on it… just the gluing, varnish and set-up. But first let us, you and I, compose a letter to a man in Berlin, the Kapellmeister of Döbbelin's theatrical troupe whose name is Johan Frischmuth. Krieger encouraged me to contact him and gave me an address."

"Why this man, Leopold? Is there not a customer in Nuremberg? Are we assured that the Berliner will buy the instrument?" She sat up straight and held both hands around her teacup like a stoic - determined to maintain normalcy in the face of potential calamity.

"There is no one here in town who is in the market for a new instrument - Krieger and I discussed it. He did mention that Mozart and one of the Bachs would be coming through town, although what I know is that they already have fine instruments. So there is only a small chance that they would want to buy mine. But, Krieger said that the Kapellmeister in Berlin might know of a possible buyer. It's someone he heard perform when he was there." Leopold didn't mention the Jew or the Jew's reputation to his wife.

Üte nodded assent.

"As soon as we finish this tea we shall compose the letter and acquire a messenger to deliver it. And, you, my excellent husband, must get to work on your creation so that we actually have a violin to sell to this buyer from Berlin."

A whiff of a smile passed over her lips, but was quickly replaced with a tight expression of worry.

He downed his drink and stood. "I'm going upstairs to change into warmer clothes, and then… to my bench with me."

He kissed the top of her head on his way up. She gathered their dishes with a measured bit of hope.

It was three weeks later when they finally heard back from Berlin. Influenza had, indeed, struck the Wilhelm home and both Üte and Leopold were caught up in the latest and most deadly Nuremberg epidemic to date – Leopold as sufferer of the dreaded affliction and Üte as nursemaid.

By some magical influence, she had avoided the current dispatch from whatever evil emissary had caused the sickness to take hold in a person. But, although Leopold grew weaker daily, he still managed each day to sit at his bench to complete one task after another.

Once the violin was glued together, Leopold attached the neck using the modern style placement that he had learned about in his father's shop. Rather than extending the neck straight out from the body of the violin - which would necessitate a wedge under the fingerboard to help the strings to reach the height of the bridge - the luthier tilted the neck slightly.

He also carved the neck the smallest bit longer and narrower than in previous models, so that musicians would have more ease when they shifted to higher positions. The new music being written for violinists required a more powerful sound, and these improvements would provide that.

As he carved the fingerboard from a slab of ebony, he lengthened it to match the neck, but waited to glue it in place until after he had varnished the violin.

Leopold worked zealously every day. In the evenings, as daylight faded, Üte lit a lantern. Then he squinted over his bench until she insisted, in the early hours of the morning, that he take some rest. He complained not at all to her about his sickness, but did not need to. Despite her best efforts and those of the physician, she watched his health slowly deteriorate over the three-week period until he became weak and pale – skeletal. Denial of the obvious was the only way she could continue on.

When the letter finally arrived, it provided the first optimism they had felt in a long time.

Üte leaned against the wall, scrolled her eyes down the page and read aloud as Leopold continued fitting a peg through its hole in the peg box.

"... Hence, I write to inform you that I have spoken with the violinist Mordechai Ben Mendel, who reports that his immediate departure from the city of Berlin is forthcoming (due to a run-in with the authorities regarding a disagreement relating to the family of one of his students. I have no further information concerning the particulars of the problem). Ben Mendel has asked me to notify you of his plans to travel to Nuremberg to assess and potentially purchase the new violin you have written to me about. If all goes as planned, he will arrive there some time during the last week of May. The man does possess means, so be assured, this will not be a frivolous venture on his part. He asked me to inform you that he will send a messenger to your door upon his arrival near the western city gate, and expects that he will be met there by you in order to transact business. He is prepared to purchase the instrument outright, for your

request of four ducats, if it suits him. However, I urge you to use caution in this matter and accept coin only; the man is a Jew, and it appears he is being run out of town. His credibility is vague, at best. I wish you and your wife safe passage through this dreadful wave of influenza and good fortune in your future endeavors. With all best regards, Johan Frischmuth."

She dropped the letter onto the bench and turned to her husband. "Well, Leopold, this is good news, wouldn't you agree? He'll be here in less than two weeks and you'll have time to finish."

The luthier set his knife down. Every movement brought discomfort, every breath was measured and faint. *So, this Ben Mendel was, indeed, a scoundrel.* He wasn't so sure that he wanted his precious violin to go into the hands of such a man. But, he was convinced that his time was short and it appeared his options were limited. In addition, he had Üte's well-being to consider. He could hardly lift his head to look at her, yet every time he did, her beauty and the spark of life in her eyes gave him comfort and courage to carry on.

"Yes, my dearest. The violin will be finished in time." *But I may be finished before it is.* "Help me lie down now for a little nap. I'll begin the oil varnish tomorrow."

"Are you sure that you want to sell to this man, this Jew? Why do you think he's being run out of town?"

She eased him onto a low counter in the shop, which they had turned into a sleeping pallet since Leopold's illness had worsened. When she offered him a sip of water, he was too weak to lift his head. His words were barely audible.

"Money is money, Üte. We'll gladly take his money if he'll give it." He coughed thinly, and then the young violinmaker closed his eyes and drifted off to sleep.

The church bell in the center of town toned six times before Leopold heard it, then sounded twice more. He cracked his eyes, saw sunlight pouring through the open shutters above his workbench, and heard the cacophony of people engrossed in barter and exchange outside the window. Dogs barked, children laughed, birds sang to their mates, and Leopold thanked God for the breath he so precariously received.

On the workbench across the small room, his stunning creation gleamed and shone in the sunlight. For weeks, by sheer force of will, he had dragged himself to the bench and, first; cooked the oils with ground resins and red pigments, then; painted layers of those oils, thinned with cedar oil, into the white wood. He had watched as the emollient miraculously brought forth beautiful patterns in the grain and stained the wood to a luminous golden brown.

Once, when he held the violin in the evening light from the window, Leopold imagined how it might have felt if, instead of a violin in his hands, he held his own son. In his vision he saw Üte glowing with pride beside him and a small, transfixed infant looking out at him through deep, thoughtful eyes. He thanked God for the apparition, for he was convinced that only in a dream would he ever behold his own child.

In his bedridden reverie, the luthier recalled his final tasks, completed only the day before; the bridge carved, strings attached and rolled onto carefully fitted pegs - then tightened into tune, the first bow drawn across those strings and the happiness in his heart at the deep, rich, resonant sounds that issued forth. He had expended his final effort to fashion a small paper label that he signed and dated: *Leopold Wilhelm, Violinmaker in Nuremberg, fecit A - 1782*, and which he then guided carefully through the f-hole with a delicate forceps and glued to the inside of the violin.

Leopold sighed – a happy and satisfied man. His only regret was that his own father would never have the opportunity to see his masterpiece. He heard their front door open and close and then Üte stood beside him with a basket in her arms. She knelt down and ran a hand across his forehead.

"Darling, I have received the message from Ben Mendel. He waits at the city gate. Shall I take the violin to him now?" Her words were balm to the dying young man. He had made it... the violin was finished.

He nodded, then a tear slipped down his cheek, which she reached out and gently wiped away.

"I know... I'm happy, too. I'll go right away."

Üte wrapped the exquisite violin in a soft, knitted cloth. Then she tenderly placed it in the wooden case that she and Leopold had selected, along with an old, well-used bow. She found the small chunk of rosin wrapped in leather and tucked it in under the neck of the violin. Then she closed the case and secured it with a strap.

Before she left, she knelt once again and hugged her husband's emaciated shoulders. With a loving kiss she left Leopold to his slumber, picked up the violin and headed down the hill toward the gate.

Part II

CHAPTER 4

Ascher Thanhausser, teacher
Jebenhausen, Germany
Nisan, 5542
April, 1782

I, Asher Thanhausser, nineteen years old, am the third borne son in a family of nine children. My father, may he rest in peace in God's loving arms, provided for our mother and my brothers and sisters in our little village near the town of Erkersreuth, a few kilometers from the border between Czechoslovakia and Germany.

Although I am happy to share some salient facts pertaining to my life, it must be understood that the story I share is not my own but that of another family and their misfortunes. I was witness to the tragic events as they unfolded and shall try to provide here a true rendering, even though nothing previous in my life or my education prepared me for the fortitude I have had to call forth from within myself in order to bear this sorrowful knowledge.

I arrived at the inn just before evening meal on a Thursday in late April. I had been walking for many days through the countryside in Württemberg, and by the time I found my way to Jebenhausen I was dusty, weary and hungrier than I had been for a long time.

My pack was considerably lighter than when I left the family I had been with near Bayreuth, for the cook's package of a quarter goose, an old apple and a dry crust of bread had lasted me only three days. I was on my second day of no food at all, save water from the lovely River Fils, and a few mouthfuls of watercress that I discovered near a spring, along with some crumbs from the bottom of my pack. My old shoes had holes worn through the soles. I had not been able to purchase a new pair for several years, as the modest pay from my work as teacher for a Jewish family near the Czech border consisted of room, board and the smallest pittance in coin which I found, to my dismay, I was unable to accumulate beyond that which I needed in order to make my journey.

By the time I reached Jebenhausen, the only money I had was that which I would use to pay my way into the protection of the village: 600 florin. I had guarded it well, though I was completely out of spending money. I had been required to pay a tax to pass through every territory and each village, and also in order to rest my head for a night in a bed. Rather than choose to sleep in the woods or under a bridge (which would have sent my mother into convulsive fits) I secured a *blett* for several nights lodging before I walked past Nuremberg, which enabled me to sleep for no payment in the homes of local village Jews along the way.

Nuremberg did not allow Jews to enter at all unless heavily taxed and accompanied by a soldier, and since there were few Jewish settlements or Jews residing in villages between there and Jebenhausen, the hunger and exhaustion which resulted from the final leg of my trip clung to me like a dog at the throat. I feared I could not walk another half-kilometer without collapse.

Some moments of my journey had been fraught with dangerous possibilities both from people and, in one instance, a ferocious hissing furry animal with a striped head and bared teeth - a badger, I believe - whose path I inadvertently crossed one evening on the side of a road. We had a startled face-to-face standoff. Then, when it lowered and flattened and hissed, I managed to back away and run before it made for me.

I was not brave and that did not matter to me. My preference had always been to seek a peaceful and quiet place; a chair placed near a window with a lovely view, a smooth stone to rest on near a gentle brook, repose under the canopy of a tree. I had a tendency toward daydreams that often provoked my father's ire and which countless times propelled me to seek shelter from the sting of his sharp words in the folds of my mother's skirts. And, although I delighted in observing God's many living creations from afar, I was happy to leave the forest and its wild creatures roaming within to the hunters.

On a lane near the fortress of Nuremberg, boys threw stones at me and yelled 'dirty Jew' and 'go home and get baptized'. I tried not to cower but did try to remain dignified, so I removed my cap and turned away and they finally stopped. After that, I kept up a lively step (or the best my energies could muster) until the last day before I reached the inn. By then, I could hardly walk for lack of food and rest. I truly feared I would stumble off into a ditch and be lost.

So, my soul gave abundant thanks when at last, I recognized in the distance what I was certain was Hohenstaufen Mountain, and below that, resting in the hills – the new village of Jebenhausen – sanctuary for my people. And, if all was to go as hoped, a steady position for me as instructor for a family's three children.

The last leg of my journey took me up the lush orchard-strewn foothills below the mountain to the edge of the old settled Christian side of Jebenhausen. On the road up the hill into town I passed a gentile farmer in his orchard and inquired of him if I had, indeed, arrived in Jebenhausen. A true thrill whipped through me when he said yes. I tipped my hat and felt light as a puppet.

I passed the Liebensteiner Castle, the church, the school and other shops. Once past the church, when I turned onto the Boller Strasse and stood to gather myself, I noticed an old man in a *yarmulke* propped-up on a short stool, leaning against the late day sun-warmed wall of a house. I waited before him and watched his pipe smoke spiral lazily upwards in the evening calm. Its smell was a comfort to me, as my own grandfather had smoked a pipe from time to time, in the evenings especially.

With his eyes shut, the old man appeared to be asleep, but I stayed because I detected awareness in his countenance. He eventually cracked an eye and leveled it at me, so I tipped my hat and bowed a little.

"*Shalom*. Good day to you, old man. God be with you."

He gave me a nod, and then surveyed me head to toe from a wary slit between his craggy eyelids. I was a sight; my tattered shoes with no stockings, my dirty jacket that was patched more than twice and bore seams across rents like battle scars, and my general overall lack of cleanliness. I had spent time earlier in the day beside a creek trying to remove some road smut. Alas, I was aware that I hadn't been entirely successful.

I waited for his response. But when it wasn't forthcoming I proceeded in Yiddish, which all Jews spoke to each other no matter where they originated or where they ended up.

"I am here to inquire about a position with the Lindauer family. A request was sent from Jebenhausen to Beyreuth for a teacher for the brother of Meyer Lindauer's children."

I didn't mention that Meyer Lindauer's brother had passed on, God rest his soul, and that I sought the family's inn where the wife of Meyer Lindauer's brother struggled alone to raise her three children and keep them in shoes and potatoes. Chances were good that everyone in the village of Jebenhausen already knew of the plight of this woman whom I had yet to meet, so I waited for the old man's response.

He slowly exhaled a weak plume of smoke, coughed a little, and then fixed his eyes on mine. As he talked, he jabbed his pipe at me like an accusatory finger.

"Mark my words, young man, that house is a hell-hole, and no one walks away from there unscathed. You watch yourself. *Kein ayin hora*."

I saw the old man shudder, and then turn his head to spit into the dust. My body's immediate response matched his… a chilling wave rushed through me. I hardly knew what to ask next.

"Why, sir? What is the nature of the problem?"

The old man turned himself so that the last of the day's weak sunshine was on him and lifted his face toward the warmth. His response was so slow in coming that I thought he had forgotten my presence or else had chosen not to reply. Finally, when I was about to move on, he began to talk.

"Well, she was a pretty little girl, no doubt about that. Everyone noticed her. She had animation. There was something lively about her even from the time she was a little one. I remember that she used to skip and sing - back in the old place!" He paused, and then went on. "How unusual to hear such a fine, clear voice in a child. And what did she sing?" He looked at me sharply, as though I should have known the answer. I shrugged. "She sang nursery rhymes and children's songs… she was just a little girl."

Who were we talking about? "The mistress of the inn?," I asked.

"Yes, her name is Chanah, lovely Chanah. But she

no longer sings." He pursed his lips and shook his head slowly from side to side. "She no longer sings..."

I asked no further questions. The old man appeared lost in reverie and at that moment my gut announced, with a slow and twirling growl, that I should move on in order to seek nourishment and rest for my weariness. I bowed slightly and touched my forehead for thanks, but he neither saw nor heard me. He sat where I had left him with his eyes cast downwards.

How good it felt to walk in the actual town of Jebenhausen - to see the candle maker's shop, a barber/butcher shop, some new houses on the Boller Strasse, a livery and blacksmith with three horses in the corral, and set back near the creek, a smaller building with a sign above the door that identified it as the ritual bathhouse - the *mikveh*.

A young man approached me with curiosity. We introduced ourselves and he directed me to the Lindauer inn, up the hill on the Vorderer Judenberg. When I finally stood in front of the inn to catch my breath, I turned and looked out over the lush valley that spread far in the distance. The sun was low in the sky, nearly set, but I could still make out fragments of the long road I had just traveled. How I had ever walked that far, I could not imagine, though my body believed that I had.

I looked a bit farther up the hill and saw two, then three women, each with her elbows askew, exit from what was surely the bake house. Each carried a heavy covered pot steaming with her family's meal, and made her way down or up the street toward home. Then, another young girl exited the same bake house with a good-sized covered kettle in one hand, leaned away from it for balance and tromped her way down the hill toward me with careful steps so she would not spill. I guessed her age to be eight or nine.

I was well acquainted with, and particularly fond of, young children. I was from a large family and had also spent time as a teacher with another prodigious family. There is something special about children pertaining to their closeness to God – to the spirit of goodness. They were so recently with Him; their innocence is unquestionable, their joy of living so magically displayed.

I looked into the girl's face as she approached and a jolt shot through me. I knew that we could not be related in any way, or at least in any way that I would know of or be able to trace, as my people lived far away and had been in that distant locality for ages. But, this child's face was as familiar to me as my own dear mother's. She looked like she could have been my sister, or my child, or a twin of myself. She had the same rounded chin as my sister, and my mother's exact mouth: those thin lips with a ready smile, that formidable nose, the tall, stately forehead, even the squared shape of her large head. But it was her dark eyes with those heavy brows, as well. Those were surely the same eyes that I had looked into every day of my life until I left my parents' home. Huge round, brown, wide-set eyes they were, that laughed and sparkled with merriment and knowing… and intelligence.

She appeared to be enjoying her walk down the hill with her heavy load. How could it be that this girl lived across the country from my home, yet seemed to me to be a close family member? I had never seen such a thing. I felt I could converse with her as easily as I did my younger sisters, and nearly did call out to her before I remembered that she was a stranger.

I stared because I could not look away, but when she came closer and noticed me, she scowled, averted her gaze, re-gathered her pot handle in both hands, turned off the road between two buildings and then disappeared.

My astonishment may have been visible, but I detected no one watching so I gathered myself and straightened my hat and jacket.

I looked directly up at the façade of the inn before which I stood and saw a cleaning rag being shaken heartily out of a high window. The shutters on all but two windows were closed against the evening's cooling air, and even as I watched, quick arms reached out and shuttered another of them.

The inn had two stories plus dormers above that. It stood with commanding presence among the new and generally smaller homes around it - solid, and for a weary and most famished traveler, inviting. A mud encrusted horse stood with its head lolling at the post next to the road. Behind one shuttered window on the first floor, the glow of warm candlelight and the sounds of dishes clanking, along with murmured voices, produced a yearning in me that brought on another loud growl from my innards.

I remembered what the old man down the hill had told me about Chanah Lindauer. But, why did she no longer sing? What had changed her? Was this family, this small world, which I was about to enter really a hellhole? Was I going to be sorry?

After such a long and arduous journey, I was willing to overlook those questions - or rather, the answers to those questions - for my stomach, legs and feet demanded a reprieve from their burdens. I could do nothing but proceed with my plan.

Before I knocked, I noticed a small iron hook embedded in the stucco with a carved wooden sign that read: Lindauer Inn. Above the letters was a *Mogen David*. I touched the *mezuzah* on the doorpost, kissed my fingers, took a deep breath and rapped the knocker.

A woman of indiscriminate age opened the door. Or rather, what I saw was a handsome, careworn woman - not yet old but appearing so, a downcast mouth with dark eyes ringed by great dusky smudges of purple and yellow-brown, like bruises. Eyes that looked out of such illuminated sockets were not unfamiliar to me. In my own family I was witness to the same phenomenon. Many of us lived our entire lives with those dark masked eyes, but perhaps with less intensity than the woman's before me. In that moment, I fondly recalled my mother's own, but caught myself and gave a small bow.

Her eyes slid twice up and down me and then met mine for a brief instant before she spoke. I was aware that I did not make my best possible impression.

"Yes?" She spoke Yiddish, of course, and her manner was curt.

"Madam Lindauer, I presume." A flash of her eyes and the smallest nod told me that she was. I bowed formally. "I am Ascher Thanhausser, a teacher for your children, sent for by a citizen of Beyreuth - from whence I have just arrived - who is acquainted with Meyer Lindauer. I have a letter…" I rummaged through my pack and handed her the sealed note.

She took the paper but did not open it, and wedged her knuckles into her hip. I saw her thoughts dash around behind her eyes, then she narrowed them at me.

"Are you one of those, God forbid, liberals who refuses to teach Hebrew? Because if you are, you can turn around right now. We're not having any of that in this house, *kein ayin hora*!" She spat a small seed vehemently onto the stone stoop beside me.

I assured her that I was qualified to teach Hebrew and had no problem doing so, but I did not discuss with her my own personal philosophy concerning reforms and assimilation. I desperately needed work and was hungry beyond words.

She glared at me for half a minute before she finally spoke. I waited.

"I have use for a teacher for my son who is to be *bar mitzvah* next year, but that is all. I will not need your services for my daughters." Her mouth tightened into a line.

We haggled over the particulars right there on the doorstep. Because I was famished and wished only to rest my bones and fill my belly, I accepted her terms without debate. I would earn an even smaller pittance than my previous meager allotment, plus I would be expected to help out in the inn. I was too weary to inquire further what that might entail. In return, room and board was to be furnished. My position as teacher would afford me two hours each morning and two hours each afternoon in tutelage with her son, except during the observance of *Shabbos* and other holidays. We shook hands and she stood aside so I could enter, finally.

Before I was escorted off to my right - into the big room - I took a look around. The building construction was nearly new - it was just five years old. And, although the ceilings were low, everywhere I looked I saw clean, modern lines supported by finely hewn timbers. A steep, narrow stairway rose from the entranceway. As I glanced up I saw a dark skirt disappear around a turn at the landing… one of the daughters, perhaps? Beside the stairs, a hall led into the back of the building and to my left, a closed door. The place appeared clean enough and there was a wonderful aroma - a mixture of wood smoke and savory cooking - that once more set off the growls and boils from within me.

How good it felt to sit again at a table. When Madam Lindauer brought me a mug of beer, I nearly threw it back for my voracious thirst. But, even though she offered, I refused a meal until I could wash up. With a morsel of time to waste, I slowly relaxed and sipped my drink. My legs tingled and vibrated and I believe, at that moment, that my hands shook. My journey was over.

I had traveled far and had finally arrived in

Jebenhausen, the place of safety - a true protected village - my own secret destination ever since I heard my father and the other men talking about it when I was younger. The idea of a place for Jews to live where they would be free from persecution took hold of my heart and did not let go until I had secured a way to make a visit there, myself.

"I heard of a village in Württemberg, bless God, where Jews aren't persecuted. They can't be forced from their homes…"

"Yeah, sure… and my uncle Chaim, may peace reign upon him, is the king…"

"No, I'm telling the truth. Izhak ben David read it in a paper. It's near Göppingen, in Liebenstein… west of Nuremberg – near Ulm."

"And they live in palaces with servants waiting on them hand and foot, may I have such a life."

"Listen, this place does exist, and the Christians helped build the town! The paper said that a letter from the Barons von Liebenstein states that their protection would not have a deadline, and, God willing, they will be safe there forever."

"…And, may health befall you all your days, you believe these lying goyim? May their names be erased!"

"I only know what Ben David said. The Jews there will be allowed to carry on with their ceremonies, rituals and festivals without persecution. It's unheard of."

"Whatever Ben David says, to me it sounds just a little bit too good to be true, kein ayin hora…"

I may have been young when I first heard about Jebenhausen - only sixteen - but I was observant of happenings around me, even then. My father and his colleagues worked every moment of their lives so that we did not starve. I often saw local gentile constables collect the Jew taxes from my father when he was trading in town or standing in his home. There was a body tax, a head tax, a tax for birth, a tax for death, a tax for pursuing a profession or trade, a tax for passing from one territory to another (different for Jews travelling on foot than for Jews travelling on horseback), a tax on livestock, and a tax to maintain wells and paths and bridges. We were also required to produce tributes to the Lords in the form of livestock, feathers, dozens of geese or other fowl. There were constant threats of eviction and harassments from officials, with regional edicts to back them up.

And, although he was a pious man, it was not in his nature to withhold his thoughts. His arguments, often made up to the heavens to an imagined judge, made sense to me: Jews were the chosen people… chosen to suffer. His problem was not that God made the Jews suffer. To him, it was the treatment of the Jews by everyone around them that bothered him so. He said that Jews were no different from everyone else, despite how those other people looked at us. He thought the old wives' tales ridiculous that turned the Jews into evildoers, out to ruin the world. He said that in his experience, Jews were, on the whole, good kind generous people. Yes, there were some who stepped outside the bounds of decency and godly behavior. But, he said, he knew *here* (and then he would pound his chest over his heart), that those kinds of people existed everywhere, among all peoples… not just the Jews. Why would anyone make laws to subjugate another people – how was that godly? When my father talked that way, I was proud to be his son.

As I drank the beer and slowly regained a bit of vigor, I looked around at my new surroundings. The main room of the inn had a corner for cooking. Next to me on a counter were bowls and baskets of food; onions, potatoes, braids of garlic, two large loaves of dark bread, and – next to them – a crock of schmaltz, vegetables in brine, several bunches of beets with withered green stems, and a good number of half-shriveled apples.

The counter ran along an inside wall and a lit hearth filled most of another. Past the counter, a door stood ajar (I could just make out beyond, a narrow back stairway and a door to the outside). The walls were plain. There were two long tables with benches and a small, square one with four chairs placed neatly around it.

No one else was in the room or entered the room

while I sat there. However, I heard footsteps above me on the next floor up so I knew there must be others nearby.

Madam Lindauer, Chanah, moved about at the counter with an uneven step. Her gait was hampered by a significant limp which caused one of her hips to ride higher than the other. From time to time she stirred up a delectable aroma from a large black pot that hung over the fire.

Her demeanor disclosed little, yet I noticed that the corners of her mouth always turned down and there was a perpetual line between her eyebrows from the scowl that attached itself to her like paint on a board. She paid me no special attention until I finished, and then with great effort, she silently guided me up the narrow turning stairs to my room on the second level.

Madam Lindauer stopped abruptly and turned toward me in the middle of the close chamber. Although I was not a tall man, she looked up at me with her evidently permanent glower.

"You will be supplied fresh water twice a day – early morning and before the evening meal. You're responsible for your own chamber pot, otherwise there is a necessary down the stairs and out the back door…." After she listed numerous directives, she paused. "Your attentions in this house are to be directed only toward my son, Samuel. Is that understood?"

I understood that she did not want me to interact with her daughters more than superficially.

"Yes, Madam Lindauer. You have my oath." I bowed slightly. She wheeled around and limped away without a word.

Before I sought rest, I sat in the chair next to the small table that would serve as my desk. It was situated perfectly to enable me to look out into the dim evening light, over the back garden of the inn to the yellowed grassy meadow beyond. Much to my great happiness, I was afforded a breathtaking vista which included forests and farmers' fields and hills that stretched far off into the distance, and I could also just make out a few establishments sitting on the higher knolls in the next town of Göppingen.

How grateful I was, finally, to lie upon the straw mattress and rest my weary legs. Fatigue overtook me and I dreamed in much cherished slumber until a sharp rap at the door startled me awake and a young voice called out to me.

"Reb Thanhausser? Dinner is served - it's time to eat!"

"Yes, yes, I'll be right there. Just one moment, please."

I hastened through my evening prayers before the meal - I was starved. I took time to throw some water on my face, combed through my hair with my fingers and descended the stairs to embrace my first encounter with the Lindauer children.

CHAPTER 5

The arrival of the music teacher at the inn precipitated momentous change. First, for good, and later… well, the story will tell. He knocked on the door nearly a month after my own initiation into the Lindauer household and immediately, the usual tenor - a somber mood that permeated the air - became infused with excitement.

All who were present at the inn that night will remember forever what the man's entrance meant in their own lives. I witnessed the children's reactions to the new guest, as the evening meal had commenced for those of us who lived under the Lindauer roof and all were yet gathered around the tables.

Samuel, the second borne and only son, a lovely curly-headed young fellow with an eager and agreeable aspect, sat at a long table along with two single gentlemen from town and myself. The old simple grandmother sat by herself at the small table. There were no others present for the evening meal that night.

Hindel, the eldest Lindauer daughter, and her younger sister Marta, helped serve the repast while Chanah paced unevenly between tables and counter like an overseer. Hindel, who kept her hair tied in a cloth and wore a dour expression much like her mother's, saw to our full cups throughout the meal.

During my first week at the inn, Hindel's demeanor presented an enigma to me. I could not understand how a young girl of such obvious intelligence could appear so bitter. Yes, it was true that Chanah, her mother, radiated a bad disposition. And, it was also true that the woman never let up on those girls; they were pressed every moment all day long to be kept busy with the cleaning, the washing, the water-fetching, the food gathering and preparation, and the numerous other chores required to run an inn and eating establishment.

But Marta, the youngest of the three Lindauer

children was as sunny and happy as Hindel and Chanah were dark. She was, in fact, the same interesting girl I had seen on my foray up the Vorderer Judenberg my first evening in Jebenhausen… the one who looked so like my own sister that my orientation was jostled whenever I saw her. After one month, I was accustomed to her bright eyes and cheery countenance, but always there were questions that niggled at me: how could it be that she looked so familiar and why were her mother and sister Hindel so persistently unhappy?

My eyes were upon Marta, as they often were, when the knock came. Her pretty head popped up, her eyes got big and round, and she quickly set her bowl down and looked questioningly to her mother. Although there was little conversation going on, everyone in the room became silent when the second knock followed.

It was not unusual to have a knock at the door in the evening, but there was a presentiment in the air that we all detected, as though whoever was there carried agitation and unknown influences along with him that would bring change to the usual and comfortable order of things. How these moments of awareness happen, I do not understand.

After a brief pause to gather herself, Chanah trundled to the door. Hindel moved behind the counter and Marta walked across the room and stood beside the hearth. She hugged herself, as though chilled, even though the room was warmed from the lit fire.

At that moment, I was impressed by the behavior of Samuel. At but twelve years old, and not yet a *bar mitzvah,* he assumed the mantle of man of the house and followed his mother to the door. He was a lad and clearly not yet a man, but his diminutive size did not prevent him from standing next to her, before the evening caller, as her protector. I imagined the shrewd perusal of the stranger by the widow Lindauer, and from where I sat I easily overheard their conversation.

"Yes?"

I recognized her customary brusqueness.

"Good evening, Madam. Allow me to introduce myself. My name is Mordechai Ben Mendel. I am a musician – I have traveled far to find a warm hearth. I have great hunger and little money. If you will allow me, I will entertain you and your guests with my violin in exchange for a meal."

The ears and interest of the children in the room perked up at the mention of entertainment. During my weeks of living in the inn, there had been no variation in the activities of an evening. The girls worked and cleaned, Samuel studied (all by lantern and candle light), and little conversation occurred. Chanah

Lindauer batted down other people's words at every opportunity and left a somber, subdued feeling in her wake.

Regardless, I enjoyed music whenever I had the chance to hear it, and was curious to hear her response to the man's proposal. It was Samuel who spoke next.

"Mother, I would like to hear this man play his violin. It has been a long time since we've heard music. Let's invite him in."

My admiration for the boy was elevated.

Another pause ensued in which I imagined Chanah's thoughts careening and colliding. She must have nodded her assent, though, because in the next moment the stranger Mordechai Ben Mendel entered the dining room followed by Chanah and Samuel.

He appeared older than my own age, that is, somewhere closer to thirty years old rather than twenty. His clothing and carriage suggested a most recent long and arduous journey, but although his attire was worn and dirty, it had once been fine stuff and was fashioned in a more ornate style than was usually seen in Jebenhausen. He set his bundle in a corner and sat down at the table.

"Well, well." He looked around at the rest of us. As he took in everything and everyone, he nodded his approval and rubbed his hands together. "A melancholy group, to be sure. Why would you be so down in the mouth? It was a beautiful day and we have a mild evening upon us. Warm weather is surely on its way. Why, I walked from near Nordingen today and had to remove my jacket in the middle of the afternoon."

He eyed Hindel as she served him a bowl, and although I would not have identified his scrutiny as salacious, he openly took in her smooth young skin, her large brown eyes and the contours of her bodice. It was none of my business, but I did offer another direction for conversation.

"You are a musician, yes?"

The stranger turned to me and looked into my eyes and I was surprised by the vibrant blueness of his own. There were few blue-eyed Jews, in my experience. When he looked at me, I thought of an icy lake on a clear day.

"Yes, I am. I am also a teacher of music."

When he said that, he glanced at Hindel, and then Marta. Of course, it was Samuel, the twelve-year-old, who spoke out.

"Can you teach someone how to play that?"

He pointed to a small black wooden case shaped disturbingly like a baby's casket, which lay with his belongings in the corner. When the musician nodded yes, Samuel spun around on his bench to find his mother. He said nothing but entreated with his eyes.

Chanah swiped a hand downward through the air, a movement that said, 'not on your life' as clearly as any words.

"There is no need for you to learn anything but your *haftorah*. We have little money enough for our daily necessities, let alone for music lessons, *kein ayin hora*." She spit a seed off to the floor and then eyed the stranger. "We do not know anything about this man, Samuel. Before anything else, we should listen to him play some music. Maybe he is not really a musician at all, but a shyster interested in filling his belly for a tale about being a musician."

I have always wondered at the prescience of Chanah Lindauer at that moment. Why any of us should have doubted the man's claims, I do not know. But, there was something suspect in his bearing, as though his forward, jovial presentation hid a part of himself that he did not want others to see. The man talked a good line for sure, and appeared somewhat refined in his eating habits. He kept up a lively banter with myself and the two other gentlemen from town who regularly followed me to the inn after *shul* in the evenings. He motioned to one of them as he chewed.

"Tell me, sir, is there a *rabbi* in this small place? I have several questions to put to him."

Mordechai Ben Mendel was a clever man. He would have us believe straightaway that he was pious.

It was a criterion, I knew, that the widow Lindauer held up as significant. If a man wanted to speak to the rabbi, it meant he desired to improve himself and his ideas. Moses Reiser answered him.

"We meet thrice daily for prayers, and longer on *Shabbos*, in our new *shul*, down on the Boller Strasse." He pointed toward it. "Our *rabbi*, who is also the butcher, is a learned man - he will help you. What, pray tell, is your concern?"

Ben Mendel ate slowly to prolong his meal while Marta and Hindel cleared away dishes from the others. A candle burned directly in front of the stranger and cast moving shadows, like dark clouds, across his face as he talked. Everyone in the room, and even the grandmother, leaned toward him so that we might better hear everything he said.

"Well, I have been places and heard things..." He peered around to make sure all eyes were on him. "There's talk of assimilation everywhere. Jews are being told they must learn the German language, and science and… literature!"

Moses Reiser turned and spat on the floor. "*Kein ayin hora*, I've heard this nonsense before. This is the wrong way for Jews to go! We will lose our Jewishness if we're not careful. Our grandchildren will not even remember how it was to be Jewish."

The other gentleman from town, a small portly

fellow who had a perpetual tic at the corner of one eye, puffed on his pipe and pounded his fist on the table.

"We don't need you to come in here and tell us what to do. We have survived centuries here without becoming German. Why would we want to be German? We are fine the way we are, as Jews first and men, second. If we assimilate, no one will be able to tell the difference between a German and a Jew!"

The musician appeared to enjoy the exchange. He threw out more bait.

"Yes, I believe that is exactly the point. When a man can no longer judge another man by the star he wears on his coat, or by his narrow scope of the greater world, then, and only then, will the Jews have achieved equality among their worldly brethren."

The pipe-smoker again pounded his fist.

"In all my years in this world, and may I live a great long life, I have never met a German who considered a Jew his 'brother'. And, the same may be said for Jews - Jews are not meant to mix with Germans. It should never happen, God forbid."

I held my tongue because I was eager to preserve my position as instructor for Samuel in the Lindauer home. But, because Samuel and I worked together every day, I had authority over what he learned. I was teaching him to read and write Hebrew as he prepared for his *bar mitzvah*. Some local men whom I saw daily at *shul* also spoke Hebrew - it replaced Yiddish for many.

I also taught Samuel how to speak, read and write German, which I had learned myself years before - although his mother was not aware of it. It seemed not only sensible, but also imperative that a young man be fluent in the language of the country that he resided in.

My old teacher who was from Berlin had studied with the learned Moses Mendelsohn. I had read many of Mendelsohn's writings and agreed with his belief that, in order for Jews to improve their lot, they must adopt, not shun, German culture.

Thus, I was an assimilationist and a lover of poetry and science and also philosophy of religion. I once read a German translation of Voltaire concerning religious dogma that produced within me a spiritual epiphany of my own. But it was necessary for me to protect my status in Chanah Lindauer's inn, so I determined on the spot to observe the conversation rather than enter into it.

The blue-eyed stranger continued. "Well, my friends, it is happening already. All around Germany, Jews are turning to books and turning away from ignorance." He waved his arms with fervor. "Young men are bridging the cultures of the Jews and the Germans. Mark my words, the Jews will have many contributions to make in the greater world because of it. And someday, Yiddish will disappear, and Jews and Germans will live with the greatest respect for each other's cultural and religious ways."

The conversation went on with each side surer of his position than the other. I held my tongue, which was not easy, because, in truth, I could not disagree with the stranger.

As the girls busied themselves with cleanup behind the counter, Chanah sat at her place next to the hearth and fed a chunk of wood into the coals. The two townsmen whispered and snorted with their heads together. The grandmother, Samuel, and I waited as Mordechai Ben Mendel carried the black wooden violin case to the table.

I admit to a trembling thrill of anticipation, for I had not heard music for many months - not since a troupe of musicians performed some rousing tunes at the market in Beyreuth. In the dim light, the shining eyes of Samuel reflected his pleasure and expectancy, as well.

When the musician gently opened the case and laid the cover back, Marta crept out from behind the counter and stood next to Samuel, just behind the shoulder of Ben Mendel. She craned her neck for a better view, hands clasped in front of her. Hindel stayed back. Ben Mendel lifted a dark colored knitted bag from the case and slid the violin out. A communal "ah" broke the silence as he held the instrument up in the light from the candle, like a prized pelt at the fair.

For many long moments he gently turned the violin and wove it through the air in the candlelight, and the golden colors in the finish gleamed and sparkled. It was, perhaps, the most beautiful artifact I had ever seen. Everyone there was struck by its luminous beauty, and none more than Marta, who stood rapt, and wrung her hands and chewed her bottom lip until I was afraid she might hurt herself. Her mother noticed, as well.

"What's the matter with you, Marta? Why all the dramatics? It's a violin, not a hundred gold coins." A small, mean chuckle escaped her.

Marta cast a brief glance at her mother but returned her attention to the violin. Samuel too, was spellbound… both children's mouths hung open. Hindel stood with an elbow on the high counter, one fingernail caught in battle with her teeth. Chanah and the grandmother both tapped a fast foot in anticipation.

My own heartbeat thudded loudly in my ears, for this was a momentous occasion. I had never been so close to a violin before and I was not alone. Despite their antipathy toward the visitor concerning his political views, even Reiser and the pipe-smoker could not help themselves - each was silent and attentive.

Ben Mendel said nothing for the longest time. He turned the thing over and over in the light, assessed its heft and rubbed his thumb up and down the back of the long, slender, smooth neck-like piece that extended off the body. It seemed that he too viewed the violin for the first time. Then he plucked the strings and turned the pegs until it appeared he had achieved an agreeable pitch for each one.

I struggle to describe that violin with enough clarity so that its beauty can be understood. It appeared new, or at least perfectly cared for, with not a scratch or a mark on it. The color, from what I was able to discern in the semi-darkness, was of a rich light golden-brown, uniformly shaded on both top and underside. Candlelight reflected off the finish as off cobblestones after rain.

More than anything else that moved me when I looked at it were the shapes: the smooth sensuous curves of the edges, the top with undulations like snowy foothills, the delicate scrolled carving at the end of the long extension piece, and the beautiful carved gashes on the top that reminded me of *f*'s, one facing forward and one backward.

Four stretched cords ran nearly the entire length of the instrument - one end of each knotted in a wooden piece at the bottom and the other wrapped around pegs at the top. The thing was delicate and splendid.

Whoever made that violin was surely a master. I felt lucky to have such an object before me.

Eventually, Samuel could no longer contain himself. "Oh sir, play something for us… please!"

Marta looked ready to burst. Her eyes were huge and round. Her hands worked one around the other like an old woman's. Every few moments she went up on her toes and down again, up and down. True to her manner, Madam Lindauer could not abide her daughter's happiness and excitement.

"Stop it, Marta, or you'll be sent out. Be like Hindel – behave yourself!"

Again, Marta paid little heed – the child was caught up in the excitement of the moment. Hindel raised her chin in superiority and assumed an air of boredom.

Mordechai Ben Mendel removed a bow-shaped stick from the case. It did truly resemble a small archer's bow, with what appeared to be long strands of fiber or hair stretched between the ends.

Slowly, he lifted the violin, placed it on his left shoulder and rested his chin on the top. His left arm reached out beneath the extension and he curved his fingers around until they were directly over the strings. Then, with his right hand he drew the bow across a string and made a sound. Marta clapped her hands and jumped up and down, and Samuel turned again to his mother with entreaty in his eyes. Chanah frowned.

"Leave me alone, Samuel. The answer is no."

Ben Mendel turned the pegs and changed the pitch of the strings for unbearably long moments. My throat dried. Marta looked as though she might be ill. Then, with no introduction, he began to create music and we were lifted aloft on a dancing wave.

The sounds ran high then low, fast slow, happy sad - all the emotions of humanity were expressed within that room so clearly that it was difficult for me to contain my own passions. I had never heard anything like it. The music I remembered from Beyreuth sounded nothing like what was before us. We heard beautiful plaintive haunted sounds, like the soul's own voice. And, as the maestro demonstrated a command of the instrument so sure and confident, a collective bubble of joy and pleasure encircled all of those present and left us suspended and spellbound.

Little Marta stood entranced, hands clasped together, as tears spilled unchecked down her cheeks. Her eyes followed every movement of Ben Mendel's; his arms, his fingers, the sway of his body. She wept openly and I can say with honesty that I understood exactly why she did. Not only was the music pleasing beyond belief, but also Mordechai ben Mendel was a sublime musician. There was not one false note to interrupt that river of miraculous sound. It was the sound of nature, of the exalted Lord God.

The old stooped grandmother folded her arms on the table and rested her head on them, and for the first time since I had arrived her face displayed a tranquil, nearly happy expression.

When the song wound its way to its destination and the music stopped, there was no movement in the room. All listened into the air as if, by listening, the beautiful sounds might remain forever. But, what I heard instead was Marta, who sobbed like a baby with her hands over her face. Ben Mendel lowered the violin and looked at the little girl as though she were an angel. His voice became gentle.

"Oh, such a tender one. Did you enjoy the music, my dear?"

Marta looked up at the musician and nodded with earnestness - her voice was nearly inaudible.

"Yes, your highness."

Well, that broke the spell and everyone in the room laughed heartily. Everyone, I should say, except Chanah. She interrupted the laughter and good feeling and I did not understand her bitterness. It was as though Marta embodied a part of her own self that she did not like to see.

"Marta, that's enough from you. Go to your room immediately and get ready for bed."

The look that the child gave her mother was

something I will never forget. Those dark ringed eyes burned into her mother's, her mouth turned down - she stamped a foot, clenched her fists.

"Noooo, mama. No! I want to see more music."

I thought it odd just then that she said "see" instead of "hear", although I did notice how keenly she had observed Ben Mendel when he performed. But, the mother was not moved.

"You go now or I'll find the switch... go on." She brushed the air with the back of her hand as though to sweep the girl away.

Marta, once again, looked up at the violinist through tear-filled eyes and clasped her hands together in front of her.

"Thank you sir, I hope you will stay. This was the best day of my life!" She turned and ran from the room, and we all heard her sniffles as she scrambled up the stairs.

Upon further conversation with Mordechai Ben Mendel, we learned that the music he played so elegantly was written by a composer named Johann Sebastian Bach - it was a Courante, from a dance suite. He told us that he had learned how to play the violin in Berlin from a renowned instructor - had spent time as an orchestral musician but now traveled as an instructor, himself. When he shared that information, Samuel lost no time.

"Oh, please, sir, show me how you played like that. I really want to learn."

Ben Mendel looked to Chanah Lindauer for permission. She stirred the fire with an iron poker and after a moment she hunched her shoulders and harrumphed.

"Eh, go ahead. What harm can it do – one time?"

Samuel stood up and waited for his lesson while the two men from town took their leave. Madam Lindauer gave instructions to Hindel, which put her sullenly back to work behind the counter. And, the old grandmother snored lightly with her head on the tabletop.

CHAPTER 6

During the following weeks, Samuel's wish was fulfilled. Mordechai Ben Mendel set up a music studio in his room on the second level that the widow Lindauer had provided in exchange for music lessons for her son, along with a weekly rental payment. Samuel began a daily study of the violin under the master's tutelage.

The boy's schedule was a busy one, as he and I worked together toward his *bar mitzvah* every morning after *shul* then again after our mid-day meal. It was late in the afternoons before evening prayers when the violin lessons occurred.

Then, early every week day morning, during his private practice sessions, the sounds of the beginner's hand were heard throughout the house. Usually the results were not terrible. Therefore, I surmised that the teacher had skill enough to direct the child toward correctness on the instrument. And, perhaps Samuel, himself, had some talent for acquiring the necessary proficiencies; that he was a quick and clever boy was aptly demonstrated during his studies with me.

Imagine the alarm of everyone when a formidable wave of influenza passed through the village and sent several to their graves. It spared those of us in the Lindauer home except for the grandmother, who laid down fevered and congested one afternoon upon her bed and expired there early the next morning.

I heard Madam Lindauer and her girls as they tended the old woman throughout the night, but to no avail. She was buried before the sun had set, along with two men and a young mother from the town who had been lost that very night, in the new cemetery off the Vorderer Judenberg at the top of the hill.

The old woman's passing had little noticeable effect on the household. There was always so much to do that could not be put off – guest rooms needed to be cleaned and bed linens laundered, food had to be gathered and prepared daily.

After several weeks, the dreadful outbreak of illness passed. When towns-people had the opportunity to evaluate the damage, it was quite uncharacteristically shown that the old and young were spared at a much greater rate than those in the middle years of their lives – even though that was not how the book of life was written for the Lindauer household. I felt lucky to be counted among the living.

Despite the good luck of having lost but only one infirm member of the family, and a mother-in-law at that, the melancholy demeanor of the widow Lindauer did not change dramatically, although I am certain that I heard an occasional hum under her breath as she went about her tasks. I would not be willing to say that she became happier, or that her countenance took on a more pleasant aspect. But, something felt different in the household due to the addition of the sounds of music in the air – there was uplift, tensions were eased, like the reflection of a welcome springtime upon the land.

I did not detect a difference in the outlook of Hindel, though. She grumbled through her days and never failed to pounce on an opportunity to berate and bully her little sister. If Hindel had a soft spot for music in her, it was not evident to me. I saw her at different moments as she passed me in hallways or on the stairs with linens in hand, or bucket and rag, or the broom, and also during meals when she served.

The girl, or should I say young woman, for she was sixteen years old, worked without pause and displayed a haughty condescension for the activities of her siblings and the lodgers in the inn. Her youthful features, which appeared pleasing initially, began to reveal the true nature of the soul within. Daily, she tightened and bristled with bitterness and scorn in what appeared to be direct response to her sister's growing happiness.

Marta was nine years old when Ben Mendel moved into the inn. She was enraptured by the violin, which so overpowered her that she suffered constant punishments for lapses in her responsibilities and chores. Daily, she leaned against the door of the violin teacher's room during her brother's lessons and practice sessions, ear to the wood, eyes shut with concentration and determination - in order to memorize every sound that issued forth from within.

I, too, occasionally paused to stand near her while we listened to master and student exchange musical phrases. Because there was but one violin, I assumed the gaps in sound were due to the need to hand the instrument back and forth between them. The bold clear, even sounds of Ben Mendel were followed by the tentative faltering attempts of Samuel, who had admirable perseverance. When I listened carefully, it was not difficult to understand every word spoken from within the room. I did enjoy the conversations between them and Marta listened even more intently than I.

"Samuel, I will reiterate once again what you must remember about making a beautiful sound: where you place the bow, how fast you pull the bow and how much pressure you exert with the bow are the key factors. If your bow slides around, your sound will be most unpleasant. And, if you press too hard with it, no one will want to listen to you! Try again. Your task is to make those strings vibrate purely, so that your sound is pure."

Samuel always answered respectfully.

"Yes, Reb Ben Mendel. It's still not easy for me to control what my bow is doing while I'm using my fingers. I work at it every day but it's difficult."

"If it were easy to play the violin, lad, then every boy in the land would do it. Keep up your practice... you're getting better."

Once, after we heard many repetitions of the same phrase, when Samuel achieved success with a particularly trying segment, Marta turned her face upward toward me. The child had eyes that penetrated into my soul - I could not look away. As per her mother's directive, I had had few exchanges with her. But, I wanted to hear what she had to say, so

I encouraged her with a nod.

"I'm so proud of Samuel, Reb Thanhausser. It's not easy to play a violin, yet he is learning every day how to make a beautiful sound, just like the teacher wants." She clasped her hands together in that endearing way and my heart was captured by her earnest appeal. "If only I were a boy, then I could learn, too."

With that, she bit her lower lip and turned her ear toward the door to listen further. Indeed, she was correct. God's choice for her was to remain the observer rather than the participant - the server, not the served. But why He had instilled a passion for the violin so devout in the child that she suffered relentlessly for it, I did not understand.

After the weeks that followed, I understood His plan even less.

As her brother's expertise on the violin increased, so did Marta's happiness. I easily recognized the girl's exuberance as she ran and skipped past me while I raked in the garden.

Gardening was the task that I had settled on with Madam Lindauer to help compensate for my stay in the inn. During several hours of each day my time was my own, and with the onset of summer, I was cheerfully willing to spend extra time outdoors.

Barring intemperate weather, I walked daily, as well, and was pleased when I located a particular path that led me through the backfields alongside an idyllic pond and old forest, and up into the Hohenstaufen Mountain pastures. There I sat under immense skies in the deep lush grasses and watched the quiet domain spread out below me as though I were the only living man.

How untroubled the world appeared from my vantage point on high. What glorious peace invaded my soul and rested there until I was bidden by duty to return to my mortal existence among the inhabitants of Jebenhausen. It was always with bittersweet reticence that I made my way slowly down the path toward the inn, to the lives and dramas that took shape there.

Late one afternoon, nearly a month into Samuel's violin pursuit, I was surprised out of my reverie on my return down from the mountain. As I neared the turn in the path that would take me past the pond, I heard someone crying nearby. With careful footing through some brambles, I made my way to the edge of the pond and found Marta seated on the bank at the water's edge.

Because of her loud sobs, she was unaware that I stood so close by. I did entertain the option of moving past unseen as the visage of Madam Lindauer's sour face crossed my consciousness, but only momentarily. The child's distress called to my heart and my humanity responded to her need.

With caution, I eased myself nearer the water and down onto the ground. I sat at what seemed to me to be a safe and permissible distance from where she was, approximately two of my own body lengths away from her. Then, I waited for her to calm herself so she could become aware of my presence.

After many long minutes, with her face hidden behind her hands, Marta's hysteria abated. Then, she pulled a cloth from her apron and wiped her eyes and nose. My concern was not to frighten her, so I cleared my throat and assumed a posture of feigned interest at something across the pond.

"Oh, Reb Thanhausser… you're here!" She was surprised but not afraid.

"Good day, Marta. I was passing by on my walk and heard you crying. What can I do to help you? Are you alright?"

She nodded her head *yes* but as she did so, more tears spilled over and ran down her cheeks. Again, she covered her face with her hands as another wave of uncontrolled emotion erupted out of her. Her shoulders heaved – I feared she might be sick.

My instincts demanded that I rush to her and hold her close, within the protection of my arms. But, for the second time in as many minutes I saw the countenance of her mother before me, so I controlled my impulse and merely waited. I say merely, but it was not pleasant to witness the anguish of this normally happy child. Spats between brothers and sisters, or even a mother's tongue-lashings, did not bring on the kind of upheaval that Marta bore as we sat on the grassy bank under the shelter of nature's canopy.

Eventually, the child's energies for grief appeared spent. She completed her ablutions and turned toward me, gathered her arms around her knees and gently laid her head upon them. Marta directed her dark gaze into my eyes and a shock of profound sorrow stung straight through me. I jumped to my feet and shook myself like a wet dog in order to rid my body of such an alien transference. Then I sat back down, prepared to hear whatever the child needed to say. She continued to stare at me but her inward vision was elsewhere. It became apparent that I must begin the conversation.

"Marta, my dear, what has happened? What is it that brings you such anguish?" More time passed. She appeared lost in a reverie of dreadfulness… those eyes. I persisted. "Marta! Can you hear me? What is wrong?"

She bit her lower lip and buried her face on her

knees, then mumbled something that I could not understand.

"What? What is it, child? Say what you must… I will not tell anyone. You can trust me, Marta… I pledge you my word."

Was that a mistake? It was a question that occurred to me then and that haunts me yet. But, the child's need was great and God had placed me in proximity to her that afternoon for a reason. "Please, Marta, share your burden with me. What is the nature of your grief?"

Before she said anything, a large raptor flew over us from behind where we sat and landed on the opposite shore of the pond perhaps thirty feet away. Marta gasped, sat up and grabbed her knees tightly. We heard the whoosh of its wings as it sailed in, and watched as it settled on the sandy shore and began to preen. What a huge bird it was - as large as a small child. Its hooked yellow beak dug around in its golden feathers and held our attention until, after a moment, it looked directly at us, cocked its formidable head and spread its wings to reveal a distance wider than I was tall. When I glanced at Marta, her eyes were locked into the bird's and the bird's were conversely fixed. Then, with a sudden whooft of uplift, the eagle's massive wings carried it aloft and quickly out of sight.

After a moment, she turned to me and spoke with

grave assurance. "Reb Thanhausser, the best thing has happened… I get to learn to play the violin." She tightened her lips together and her eyes moistened again, which confused me.

"Well, Marta, that sounds very good. Are you not happy about this?"

She nodded solemnly. "Yes, I'm happy about it. I had my… my first lesson this afternoon." She looked away, across the pool.

I could not understand the incongruence. "Is it your mother? Is she forbidding you from learning to play?"

The child flashed me a severe look. "No sir. She doesn't know yet. I think she would not allow it." Marta pulled a long piece of grass from the ground and twirled it in her fingers. She was quiet.

I, too, was silent for several minutes. It was pleasant out there beside the water. We could hear the wind blowing mildly through the early summer leaves, and small birds and insects flitted about, oblivious to our presence. Marta rocked like a man praying but made no motion to leave, even though it was nearing evening mealtime when her absence from the inn would be noticed.

If her mother was unaware that she was to learn the violin, then the child feared the woman's wrath and held a worrisome secret, which I knew was not easy on a person – particularly a child. Whether Madam Lindauer wanted me to interact with her daughter or not, I decided just then to do whatever I could to assist Marta. After all, if she was not my own sister, she looked enough like her that my heart told me that she was, in spirit. I encouraged her again to unburden herself.

"I should like to hear you play the violin before long. Will you tell me how you came to take a violin lesson? Hmm? Did you ask Reb Ben Mendel if he would teach you?"

She spoke slowly, with none of her usual vitality. "No, I did not ask him. He asked *me* if I wanted to learn to play the violin. I was sitting on the floor outside the door during Samuel's lesson. You know... where I usually sit?"

"Yes, I know where that is. Go on." I nodded encouragement. It was good to hear her begin to open up.

"Then, before Samuel's lesson was over, the door opened and Reb Ben Mendel found me there. I didn't ask him to teach me... I didn't! I was... was afraid because I thought he might not like that I was there, by the door." She turned fully toward me, which I took as a good sign.

"So, what did he say to you, Marta? Was he angry?"

"Oh no, he asked me if I wanted to go in to the room. And, then I said *yes* and he invited me in and closed the door. Samuel was in there, holding the violin." When she spoke the word violin, her voice became reverential and she clasped her hands together in her lap. "I got to sit in the corner and watch the rest of Samuel's lesson. Reb Thanhausser, I got to watch him learn how to slur notes together with his bow!" Animation crept into her story. She became excited.

"Well, how did it happen that you, yourself, received a lesson?"

With my question, her demeanor transformed. Whereas moments before, her aspect was bright – suddenly she darkened. She straightened both legs out before her and smoothed her skirts over them, repeatedly. I asked the question again, and eventually she answered.

"Reb Ben Mendel asked me if I would like to learn to play the violin. He said he could give me a lesson right then." She paused, so I nodded for her to continue. "I looked to Samuel to see what he thought and he told me that Mama would not like it. I knew that, too, but I want to learn to play the violin more than anything… anything. And, Samuel knew that. We've talked about it a lot."

The girl became agitated as she spoke. She knocked the toes of her shoes together and rubbed her hands vigorously down her skirts. I was patient and said nothing.

"Then Samuel said that he would give up some time during his lesson so that I could have my own short lesson but that we mustn't let mama know. He said he would do his best to guard the room while I have my lessons and that mama, who doesn't pay that much attention anyway, would hear me and think it was him. It made me so happy I thought I would burst."

I wondered how long it would be before Madam Lindauer uncovered their deception. I hoped there would be enough time for Marta to become proficient on the instrument. In my opinion, any person – even a girl – who felt that much passion for something ought to have the opportunity to fulfill their desire.

Of course, I usually found myself on the side of the argument that favored the underdog, the oppressed, and in the small hamlet of Jebenhausen, not always with victorious results. In the Lindauer household, it was often imperative that I held my tongue. Now I would have yet another reason to do so.

The afternoon waned, but I wanted to hear all that the child had to say. I stood and offered her a hand. "Come, Marta. We should make our way home. Your mother will be upon you yet again, I fear."

She took my hand and pulled herself up, and we

began our twenty-minute walk together down to the village. For most of the distance she kept her arms wrapped tightly around herself, as though she was chilled. But, the warmth from the day had not abated and I found it necessary to sling my jacket over my shoulder to remain comfortable.

The path widened as we passed alongside fields, some planted, some which lay fallow with last year's grasses – folded and windswept in waves and furrows. We watched a blackbird balance on one slender stalk as it bobbed and swayed in the wind.

Marta said nothing until I queried her again. "So, you had your first violin lesson then? How did it go for you?"

Nearly a minute passed before she answered. I glanced over at her and was startled to find her deep in thought. She looked like a worried old woman... a crone, instead of the nine-year-old girl that she was. When she finally began to talk, she spoke slowly and chose her words carefully.

"Reb Thanhausser, he… I… he said… he… he…" She struggled to communicate something, and then appeared to move past that thought to another. "When I held that violin, it was the best moment of my whole life. And after he showed me how to hold the bow and pull it across the strings, I couldn't believe it. I actually played the violin... I get to learn to play music!"

Clasped hands, great happiness.

But tears appeared, yet again, in her eyes. Were they tears of joy? I could not tell. Those same tears spilled down her cheeks as she continued.

"Samuel went out and stood outside the door, to guard for mama. The teacher, he said... he said..." She covered her face with her hands, but could say no more.

Unease coursed through me. "What did the teacher say, Marta?" She was alone in the room with the man! Her mother would perish from the thought *kein ayin hora*. "What did he say to you?"

Marta stood beside a boulder in the day's last sunshine. Her diminutive size in the landscape's vista belied the true nature of her determination. She folded her arms in thought and then appeared to come to a decision. With the back of her hand, she wiped away her tears and answered me with resolve.

"He... he told me that I did very well. We made a deal. If I do not tell mama... *anything,* he will teach me all there is to know about how to play the violin." She raised her chin in the air defiantly. "And, that is the best thing that could ever happen." She turned to me and fierceness flashed in her dark eyes. "You promised you would never tell, Reb Thanhausser!"

What could I say? Indeed, I had made an oath to her.

I remembered with a wince that I had also made an oath to her mother. I was at a moral crossroads and I chose, in an instant, to help this beautiful troubled child who stood before me. As unsettled as I felt, as uneasy as I was about the subversion, my own conscience required that I be true to Marta… the vulnerable one.

"Yes, my dear, I promise. Your secret is safe with me." *God help us all,* I thought, as we made our way back to the inn, to the fates that awaited us in destiny's hands.

CHAPTER 7

There cannot be enough said about the glorious beauty that God bestowed upon our corner of the earth during that summer season. After the epidemic's dark days throughout winter and spring, which lingered for weeks beyond what was reasonable by any account, the soothing warmth and long slow days that summer brought were a balm to the sensibilities of everyone in our little enclave.

All of nature raised a toast to the rebirth of the world. Never had I seen so many fawns skitter joyfully beside their mothers, or heard the chatter of so many winged creatures across the fields. Flowers of every hue bloomed in profuse luxuriance alongside paths and roadways, as if they sang their own songs of happiness to the Lord. Even the green branches of the tallest trees lifted and waved their arms in joyous celebration of existence.

I found myself out-of-doors at every possible opportunity. It was always a relief to walk out of the inn to find the fresh, sweet air that awaited me past those walls.

The garden began to show signs of potential abundance, as the small green shoots stood up in straight rows, like good children. Peas climbed their trellis, then blossomed. Squash began their slow crawl over the soil. I cannot fully explain the happiness I felt every time I coaxed an unwanted weed from its secure stance and felt that particular instant when it released from earth's tenacious hold and came forth in my hand. The sun on my back, the insects' hum, the wind through my beard, all restored me and gave me hope ... hope for the future. Hope that the inexorable passage of time would deliver a solution to the intricate web of difficulty that was evolving at the Lindauer inn.

As the summer proceeded, so did the children's progress with their prospective endeavors. Samuel did not appear to be affected by the season as I was.

His pallor remained winter pale as he spent long hours indoors with his *haftorah*, his Hebrew studies (as well as German), and the violin. Aside from myself at a younger age, I had never seen a more driven child. He told me that his father, may he rest in peace, passed away when Samuel was a small boy - soon after Marta was born - and that he always knew that it was his duty to work hard and make something of himself. He had few options as the son of an innkeeper, so he was determined to learn as much as he could in order to please God and the memory of his father.

I spent many mornings in the garden with hoe in hand listening as Samuel, and Marta, too, practiced their music lessons. It was but a matter of weeks before I was unable to discern which child it was who played upon the instrument. Then one afternoon, I was amazed to discover that it was Marta's music I favored when I looked up toward the window and saw Samuel there, with no violin in hand, and heard lovely music that delighted my heart flowing from the room behind him.

Those hours spent by Marta with her ear to the door of Samuel's lessons were not time spent in vain. The girl had abundant facility - more than her brother, I dare say. The sounds she brought forth, even as a new beginner, were sweeter, richer and more confident than Samuel's own.

Their deception held. Obviously, no one else was aware that Marta spent time alone with Mordechai Ben Mendel daily, and it was still a secret that she practiced regularly, as well. I often passed Ben Mendel's room to find Marta at her place outside the door as she listened with intense focus to what transpired on the other side. And less often, I spotted Samuel there, always with a book in hand, as he guarded for his sister.

We had a conversation early in the summer wherein I explained to him that I was aware of their duplicity, but also was in favor of it. Whenever Samuel's eyes met mine in that hallway, we shared a secret and a common unease. I knew that he was happy for Marta, but anxious about the day they would be found out by their mother. *Kein ayin hora*, it would not be good.

Alas, the day we had all dreaded for many months finally arrived on a humid airless August afternoon. And, it was not Chanah who made the discovery. It was Hindel, the eldest and most irascible of the three Lindauer children. Due to a bit of good luck, Marta had several months of lessons and practice behind her when she was found out.

Considerable tension and unease permeated the

hallway outside Ben Mendel's room when, by unfortunate coincidence, Hindel passed through, arms laden with folded bed linens, and found Samuel and myself engaged in conversation. Why the unlucky conjunction had not occurred previous to that moment, I do not know.

She easily heard the unmistakable sounds of student and master that emanated from behind the door. My heart lurched and throbbed violently, my throat went dry. The young woman's expression said more than words could. An eyebrow shot up, then she squinted and sneered at her brother.

"Well, well. What have we here? Is that who I think it is in there?"

Samuel was unruffled as per his usual demeanor. For a twelve-year-old the boy had composure beyond his years. He folded his arms and stood up straight. Although he had not yet achieved his full height, he did have several inches on his sister and used them to good effect at that moment.

"Hindel, you must not tell our mother about this. Marta is…"

But, Hindel was not swayed. "Is she in there alone with Reb Ben Mendel? Are you serious? I'm going right now to tell mama. This is scandalous!"

She turned to go down the stairs but Samuel intercepted her in the hall. He grabbed the bundle of bedding from her arms and tossed it to the floor. Then he blocked her way with his body.

"Listen to me, Hindel. Listen..."

She was not to be convinced of anything, however. With no warning, she turned back, pushed the handle down and shoved open the door to Ben Mendel's room. Then she lurched in with Samuel directly behind. I paused at the doorway and witnessed what happened from there.

Marta's face reflected pure horror. Her eyes widened into large black orbs that fastened onto her sister's. Her mouth dropped open like a rabid animal. In an instant her skin blanched grey, then she backed away from the music stand near where Ben Mendel stood, and lingered beside the window.

The violin was tucked up under one arm; she had one hand secured around the neck, another held the bow. Before a word was spoken her chin went up in a defiant stance, but she trembled perceptibly. I had such a rush of empathy for the child just then that I nearly intervened on her behalf. However, personal discretion interceded, so I held myself back.

Hindel thrust her hands upon her hips and, from my vantage point behind her, she resembled her mother exactly. When she spoke, she so imitated the woman that, had my eyes been closed, I would have thought it was the widow who bellowed with that coarse and abrasive voice directly at Marta.

"What do you think you're doing, Missy? You are in so much trouble." It was easy to detect the acerbic delight in those words.

The teacher, Ben Mendel, stood with his hands folded, sheepish and meek. He said nothing, but there was a glimmer of amusement in his eyes, as though the significant tribulations of these children were but sport to him. A flash of dislike toward the man passed through me. I was, at that moment, unaware of how much more that feeling would be amplified within me in the future.

Samuel wasted not a second. He moved between the sisters and faced Hindel.

"Hindel, you can't tell mama. This must remain a secret. You know very well that she would never allow Marta to continue with Reb Ben Mendel. You know it." The boy's face twisted with emotion – he held back tears but continued valiantly. "Marta is… she's so good at this. Hindel, she has a gift from God!"

The older girl threw her head back and laughed a great guffaw. "A gift from God? What a ridiculous thing to say, Samuel. This is no gift, this is just wrong. Wait 'til mama hears about this!" She shook a finger at her little sister. "You're really going to get it, Marta."

Then, she looked at Ben Mendel and assumed an air of authority. "I don't know what you think you're doing, sir, but this is absolutely inappropriate. My mother will know about this directly, so I suggest you prepare yourself." She folded her arms and gazed imperiously upon her subjects.

Everyone was stunned into silence. What little air there was went out of the room and for a moment I thought I might crumple from the heat. Rivulets of perspiration trickled down Samuel's temples. The shirt Mordechai Ben Mendel wore bore large dark ovals where it was dampened through. How those girls maintained their composure in that humid hothouse under so many heavy garments was a mystery to me – and Hindel wore a head cloth, as well.

It was Samuel who broke the charged quiet.

"Before you tell her, Hindel, why don't you listen to Marta play the violin. You'll see for yourself how good she is."

Hindel sneered back. "How *good* she is, how *good* she is. Do you think I care how *good* she is? I do not, Samuel. And, you… little miss wonderful… don't think you're going to get away with this." The young woman hissed those words like a viper. I had never seen her so vehement, so hateful toward her sister.

Marta's eyes floated in liquid. She bit her lower lip, lifted the violin and secured it under her chin, then set the bow upon a string and began to play. Although it was a simple dance tune, even the air around us became lively and animated. The sound permeated the heavy atmosphere like it was borne upon magic, with richness, lightness and energy from the spirits.

It was as though the instrument spoke directly from her soul to mine. Such pure sound, pure and innocent and beautiful and glorious. I wiped a surreptitious tear. Never had I heard such a thing, ever. And from a child! Even the music of Mordechai Ben Mendel did not speak to me the way those dancing notes did.

When the music ended and the final echoes were carried off into the distance, we found ourselves, once again, in the music teacher's room with an immense problem yet unresolved.

Marta slowly lowered the violin and gazed out the window. Then she closed her eyes and hugged the violin to her, as a mother would its dearest babe.

Did that experience soften the heart of Hindel? If so, Samuel allowed no time for a capitulation to her previous conviction.

"See, Hindel? We must protect her, not chastise her. She has a gift – she should continue to learn. She's a much better musician than I am on the violin… much." He looked over at Marta, who watched them gravely. Her fingers worked silently up and down on the fingerboard.

Hindel said nothing, which I took as a good sign. Ben Mendel was mute, as well, for which I was thankful. I did not wish to hear his opinion just then. Samuel pressed on.

"Hindel, what would it take for you to keep quiet about this? Marta, would you be willing to take on one of Hindel's chores as a way to keep her from telling mama?"

The older sister interrupted shrilly. "She's already slacking on her chores. I've had a lot more to do lately and now I know why!"

From her tone, I would not have been surprised to see her stick her tongue out at Marta, but she merely folded her arms in that haughty way she had.

"Why shouldn't I tell mother? This is unbelievable!" At least she questioned whether she should tell or not.

It appeared Samuel had made some headway with his offer. He wasted no time. "Now that you know about this, Hindel, we can work something out, right Marta?"

Everyone looked at the small girl who had backed herself into the corner. She flicked an anxious glance toward her violin teacher, and then looked in my direction. That child held something immense inside of her – a thing that made her precious and rare. Why had God given such talent to a girl? I marveled at the mysterious ways of the Lord.

As an ethical man, I could not deny the emotion

within that compelled me to protect her, to cherish her the way her brother Samuel did. I hoped my words provided comfort to her.

"Your secret is safe with me, Marta. You know that."

Hindel snorted with scorn. "I guess I'm the last one to know anything around here. Humph!"

It took nearly half a minute for Marta to articulate her answer. Several times she looked at Ben Mendel but he appeared to be engrossed in some papers on his desk. I wondered at the man's *chutzpah*. He knew he defied the orders of the house, yet he showed no compunction for his actions.

Disquiet shivered through me when I remembered that I, too, defied Madam Lindauer daily as I provided lessons in German for Samuel. My harsh judgment of the man was, perhaps, misplaced. In my defense, I will say that Samuel's success in the future was dependent upon his ability to carry on business with those in the greater world. Times were changing between Jews and Gentiles in Germany, and I felt it necessary to prepare him.

But, it was wrong for Ben Mendel to jeopardize Marta's wellbeing, though she obviously had a gift that cried out to be nurtured. If he understood Chanah Lindauer even somewhat as well as I did, then I was not surprised that he had failed to go to her for permission to teach the girl. When it came to Marta, the widow Lindauer bore significant antipathy.

In more than four months of observation, I never saw her deliver a kindness in Marta's direction. There was an understanding between Hindel and her mother that apparently surpassed the need for thoughtfulness. They were both focused on the myriad tasks that comprised the running of the inn.

Samuel was Chanah's golden child. Hence, toward him she had an altogether different approach and manner.

But, sweet Marta (and the girl did possess an agreeable and perceptive disposition) earned only condemnation and reproof from her mother and sister, no matter what she did. Ben Mendel was right to spare Marta from her mother's wrath, yet wrong to be her violin teacher in the first place. Such a dilemma for all, *God forbid,* I had never seen.

At last Marta turned to face her sister. "I will take over all the chamber pots and all the inside cleaning duties. I will also get back to all of my tasks that I have slacked off on lately. And," she tightened her mouth and paused before she finally made up her mind, "I'll clean the privy from now on, too."

I assumed those were chores that Marta knew her sister found abhorrent. I certainly would have.

The very ether in the room shimmered in the late

afternoon heat as we waited to hear Hindel's response. That she had been made an offer she would be hard pressed to refuse was obvious. Her toe tapped nervously and her mouth drew sideways in an unsightly fashion as she chewed on the membrane inside. Marta's eyes never left her sister's face. By the time Hindel uttered her answer, little air remained in the room. Her words had edges like knife blades.

"If you fail to carry through on what everyone here heard you say you will do, I'm going immediately to our mother to tell her, do you hear me?"

Marta narrowed her eyes. "I'll do what I say I will do, Hindel. But, you have to be true to your word, too."

The older girl flipped her hand as she turned. "Ha, you pathetic little liar - we'll see who's true to their word!" She glared at Ben Mendel and then, before I had a chance to move aside, she pushed past me through the doorway, gathered up the bundle of bedding and tromped down the stairs.

Mordechai Ben Mendel responded swiftly. He straightened the music on the music stand and motioned for Marta to resume her place before it. Then he bowed to Samuel and myself.

"The girl's lesson has not been completed. We need more time to…" he cleared his throat, "… to finish." He turned his back to us and proceeded to speak to

Marta as though we were invisible, so we left the room and Samuel shut the door behind us.

In the hallway, he clasped his hands together. "Whew. That was *really* close." I nodded assent. "I know we shouldn't deceive our mother this way, but you heard Marta play. There's something special about the way she makes music - she has a magnificent gift."

"I cannot disagree with you about that, Samuel. She makes the violin come alive. But, we are all complicit in this dishonesty and I fear that no good will come of it. Your mother will have all our hides."

Samuel hung his head. "Yes, I know. It seems important, though. I feel Marta must do it - not just that she wants to do it, but that she *must*."

The boy and I stood in the stifling hallway for nearly ten minutes as we discussed the subject of his sisters and mother. Sometimes it was not easy to remember that he was a youth of twelve, for he had a keen understanding of human fallibility. I wanted to continue our conversation but I needed air.

Even after I left him and sought the nominal breeze of the garden, I failed to recognize a most salient fact. It was not until months later, as many ugly truths unfolded, that those moments came back to me. During the entire time that Samuel and I stood in the hallway, on the other side of the door from where

Marta ostensibly completed her violin lesson, not a sound emanated from within… not one sound.

CHAPTER 8

The end of summer passed. We prayed to have our names inscribed in the book of life for another year, and entreated the Lord to have our sins be forgiven.

My conundrum was about the nature of sin: the question of whether my collusion with the Lindauer children actually constituted a sin in the eyes of God. I exercised free will in making the choice to help conceal Marta's activities, yet I could not bring myself to see my violation as an evil.

Neither could I describe what I did as a lapse in morality. What moral man would not step forward to procure protection for Marta, who most certainly possessed the tendency of musical genius? She was a girl and poor at that, which made my actions even more essential.

Girls' lives were circumscribed within the boundaries of home and hearth where, for most, education of any kind was not encouraged. Few families chose to educate their daughters; Chanah Lindauer adamantly opposed it.

I knew deep within my own soul that my complicity was the correct option for Marta, yet I steadfastly concealed my behavior from her mother and every other person in the village. Why? Why, if I knew it was the right thing to do, was I loath to have anyone know that I did it? Did my involvement fulfill the true meaning of a *mitzvah*, an act of human kindness that required anonymity in the doing? How could it when Hindel, Samuel, Marta and Ben Mendel were fully aware?

If we were commanded by God not to pursue the passions of the heart, did that mean that Marta sinned when her heart's fervor was displayed, as her fingers and arms moved in time with powerful unseen forces in order to bring forth such glorious sound?

Whenever I sought clarity, I encountered mystery.

How could my Lord punish me for doing something that, from deep within my innate humanity,

I was compelled to do? My very little solace came from the knowledge that, in truth, all people sinned at various points in their lives. I was also somewhat comforted by my unremitting hope that God tempered justice with mercy.

In preparation for the harvest and my favorite autumn holiday of *Sukkos*, I constructed a small tabernacle in the garden made of sticks and branches gathered from the forest. Marta, Samuel and I hung gourds, apples and pears from the rafters with twine and brought in fresh cut wildflowers.

How lovely it was to stand together under the heavens and praise the Holy One for giving us life and protection in the village of Jebenhausen. Each day and night for seven days, we partook of our meals there, at a table that we moved outdoors from the inn.

In the evenings, after a meal and prayers, Samuel and Mordechai Ben Mendel took their turns on the violin. They played festive music that we danced to, albeit more simple strains from Samuel, as well as plaintive melodies that made us remember the suffering of our ancestors who wandered in the desert for forty years. We had much to be grateful for.

Marta appeared to enjoy the music, but her overall vivacity was diminished. I was puzzled by her fading enthusiasm for life, which was in contrast to the lively girl I remembered from when I first arrived at the inn in the spring.

All through the autumn her eyes gradually lost their luster, her cheeks their rosy radiance, until she took on a tightened, drawn aspect that, regrettably, resembled her mother. She no longer went about with that twinkle in her eye or a happy song under her breath. Instead, she plodded through the days with her head down, and failed to look into anyone else's eyes, including mine. It troubled me to observe the decline of her spirit.

I knew that she continued to progress on the violin, though, as I heard extraordinary strains issue forth during her lessons and practice periods. Samuel gave over a majority of his time with Ben Mendel so that Marta might benefit from more instruction with the teacher.

And, for inexplicable reasons, Chanah Lindauer did not suspect the deception that her children carried on directly under her nose, although I noticed that the children's morning practice sessions often coincided with their mother's outings to the market, and she almost never climbed those stairs.

I heard the widow brag many times to guests of her son's prowess on the instrument. It was routine for Samuel to be asked to perform after dinner. He always complied, but it was an enigma to me why Madam Lindauer did not notice the difference between the splendid music of Marta's that filled the house during the day and the lesser quality presentations that her son produced in the evenings.

The real puzzle to me, though, was why did Marta appear so unhappy? Her gladness should have grown in parallel to her skill acquisition, should it not?

One late autumn afternoon after *Sukkos* had passed, as I stooped between two rows of yellowed carrot-tops in the garden, Marta stepped over the leafy patch of potatoes, crouched onto the dirt beside me with a shawl over her bowed head and waited in silence. We heard Samuel's violin from a window above, but I did not know at that moment where her mother was. Marta leaned closer toward me and whispered.

"My mother is out."

I waited several moments so she might explain why she was there but she remained still, so I busied myself with the last of the carrots - pulled and placed them in the basket - and then turned my head to look at her. When she peered up at me from under her shawl, my heart constricted until I coughed. Those large brown eyes, the ones that had caught my attention on my first day in Jebenhausen, were now sunken and ringed with layers of dark purple and brown, like bruises. Her skin was pale, which made the severity of her shaded eyes even more pronounced. She had been crying, and still was, although she made no sound. She looked directly at me and held on. Never had I felt such an intimate jolt.

"What is it, my dear? Why do you weep?"

No response, just the intensity of her stare into my own heart. What could possibly produce that much anguish in a child? I set down my trowel, wiped my hands on my apron, and looked around us. It appeared that we were alone, but anyone might come around the corner of the inn at any moment.

I could only surmise that the weight of her deception had become too much to bear. Perhaps it was time to tell her mother of her deceit so that she might be free from the burden of such a scheme.

"Please tell me, Marta, what I can do to help you. It is most disturbing to see you so upset."

She motioned to me to follow her out the back gate and onto the path that we had walked together in the spring. In a moment, I removed my apron, placed it in the basket beside the gate and followed her.

It was clear to me that, aside from Samuel, the child had no friends - her mother saw to that. On occasion, Marta left the house to visit the market, or to deliver or collect a pot of food from the bake house, or to run a quick errand. The girl's movements were controlled and I knew she had no one else to turn to.

Because she chose to confide in me, I felt a familial duty to respond. We were not related, as far as I knew, but in my heart of hearts, Marta was my sister - as surely as if the soul of my own sweet departed little sister, Merriam, had appeared in the form of nine-year-old Marta Lindauer. She stirred questions and feelings of protection deep within my breast. I wanted to help her.

Before we progressed up the path as far as the pond we turned onto a small, nearly undetectable tract that took us through some brambles into a copse of long-needled pines. They were old trees with magnificent dimensions. It would have taken four men of my size, one on top of another, to reach the lowest of the branches. The ground was covered with a carpet of discarded pine needles which muffled our steps, and the air was mild and still.

Marta led me around the base of a giant old beech tree where she pointed out a hole in the trunk large enough for a child to climb into.

"Samuel and I used to come here to play - before you came, Reb Thanhausser. We pretended that this place was heaven, and would hide us from… from our mother, and Hindel, too." Her shoulders drooped. "Now, all he does is study and practice the violin."

I understood why the children loved the hidden

clearing. It was the sort of place that I, myself, might have retreated to as a youngster – away from the constant noise and activities of our lively household.

She sat on a small knoll beside the gash in the tree, removed the scarf from her head and looked at me again with her anxious eyes. I sat nearby and waited.

"Reb Thanhausser, I want to tell you something. I *must* tell you... Reb Thanhausser... I am... I am..." Before she could finish, tears arrived – she broke down and wept.

In truth, I was not surprised at her disintegration. What child could hold up under the weight of such devious subterfuge? I waited for her to gather herself, and then tried, with utmost care, to coax her story forth.

"Marta, dear. You know that I have carried your confidence with me all these months. I have divulged to no one what you have given to me to protect. Since we spoke last, I have shared only with Samuel about what is going on."

Her chin trembled and she nodded. "Yes, Reb Thanhausser. You're good at keeping a secret. Thank you."

She appeared somewhat calmed so I continued.

"You know that you can talk to me, don't you?" An affirmative nod. "Can you tell me what is troubling you so? Hmm?"

She mumbled something, but because her head hung before her, I was unable to make out her words.

"Marta, what did you say?" I reached out and gently lifted her chin with one finger but she pulled away. "Tell me again what you said... please?"

Although she still had trouble with the words, I did hear her.

"I try to be good... I do! But really, I'm bad... I'm *bad,* Reb Thanhausser, so, so *bad.*"

She covered her face with her hands and heaved with grief. Her distress was formidable, yet I could do nothing but bear witness. I knew better than to offer my arms for consolation so I lingered while she composed herself.

The trouble with a lie was that the disagreeable repercussions from the invention of a fabrication always fell squarely on the liar. I had witnessed the scenario many times as a youth. One of my brothers was born with the compulsive inclination to fashion exaggeration to the point of dishonesty. I watched my parents scold and punish him, but to no avail. The trait was inborn in the fellow and would, I was certain, accompany him to the grave.

Marta, however, was not a liar. And the cost to her for harboring untruths was being manifest before me beneath those majestic trees. I sought patience and kindness.

"I cannot see you as a bad person, Marta. You say you are bad, yet truly you are not. Just because you secretly play the violin, that does not make you bad. Surely God does not believe you are bad." In truth, I did not know what God believed. "I can see that this lie is having an adverse effect on you. Might it be time to tell your mother about your deception?"

She shoved her knuckles against her mouth, shook her head with vehemence from side to side. "No! Don't do it! You don't know… everything, Reb Thanhausser. He… he… I am punished - I am bad. I will never grow up. I'll never be a good wife or mother…" More tears, more upheaval.

He? Why had she said *he*?

A jagged tremor convulsed down through me and left me shaken and sick. Was there more to her anguish than I knew? A man? *Gott im Himmel,* she was upset about a man? I had to know.

"Who is ***he***, Marta! Who are you talking about?"

There was only one *he* in Marta's life other than Samuel and myself. A dark nefarious cloud mushroomed within me.

The anguished child studied my face. Although stricken, I returned her look with my best imitation of calm, and we sat for several long moments until she shuddered and drew in a quick breath.

"You promised you wouldn't tell anyone, Reb

Thanhausser. You can't tell on me ... you promised!"

"That's right, Marta. I will honor your confidence. I am a man of my word – you have nothing to fear."

She was only a child, but I felt as pinned to my oath as though she were an emissary of God and I, the supplicant seeking entrance to heaven. A fearful premonition flew into me and flapped around. It left my throat dry and my heart clenched. I did not want to hear the words I feared she would say.

In the instant before she spoke, all movement and sound ceased within the grove. An ominous pressure filled the space around us. No bird sang, no breeze rustled through the high branches. Only one small beetle climbed out from under some pine needles and pulled and slipped its way along. The quiet where we sat was so complete that I distinctly heard the sound of the insect's scratches as it struggled to move forward. I swallowed to try to ease the pressure inside my ears.

Marta laid her head against her knees, her shoulders trembled. I heard her murmur but the words were not clear.

"You spoke of a man, Marta. Tell me who he is. Tell me what is bothering you so." Although I spoke quietly, my heart thundered in my chest.

She looked up at me with fear upon her face. Her dark eyebrows furrowed into a ridge, her chin quaked.

"I can't say... I *can't*." She bit her lower lip and

entreated me through tear-filled eyes.

In truth, I had never found myself in such a profound circumstance. I had watched my little sister die, as well as my own father and grandmother. But, being present at each of those passages precipitated a sad peacefulness rather than what I dreaded Marta's declaration would produce.

The gravity of her stare, and my own trepidation over what I was about to learn, rendered me helpless – at the mercy of God – and I could do nothing but listen to her confession and then carry that burden within myself. Still, she appeared unable to utter a coherent response.

"Do you wish me to ask you? Would that make it easier for you?"

An affirmative nod.

"Alright, then. Is it...?" My God, it was difficult for me to say. "…Reb Ben Mendel?"

I could not breathe for several seconds before she responded. Finally, one moment before I thought I would burst from the burden of the wait, she produced another small assenting nod. Then, she laid her head on her knees and I watched, stricken, as her small body shuddered and heaved. I did not touch her or offer her comfort of any kind.

An instant vision of the man came to me. I saw his hands, those clever hands with their clawing fingers reaching for Marta, and then I leapt up from where I sat and tramped around to dislodge the unbearable image.

As I paced, I heard the words from Genesis repeated over and over in my mind: "*the imagination of man's heart is evil from his youth.*" A heavy moan roared from my chest. My agony was so great that I threw my arms about and nearly tore at my lapel.

For many long moments, I was lost in a storm of temper... until I finally remembered that my own outrage was not the issue. It was the child who required my attention.

I returned to her side, knelt down and leaned gently toward her. I used great restraint not to gather her close and preserve her safely within my arms.

"Marta, my dear, are you harmed?" I quaked from the exertion of my outburst and from such images as had begun to take hold in my imagination.

Marta swiped an arm under her runny nose and squinted at me through reddened, swollen eyes. A more wretched child I had never seen. I repeated my question.

"Are you harmed in any way?" If she would say no, then I would be able to breathe once again.

Her mouth formed a crooked, determined line, but she said no more. She looked at me through those eyes as though I had the answer she needed, as though I could say what she could not. But, I was speechless.

What does one say to a nine-year-old child after an admission such as hers? Was I a fool to believe that she might yet remain unharmed? If her present distraught condition in the woods was any indication, my question was moot. She *was* harmed. How, then, to proceed?

We stared into each other's eyes and I saw pain and fear lodged within her alongside her keen intelligence. Also, I detected something like hope as she bore into my soul and, without a spoken word, demanded fulfillment of the vow I had renewed vigorously only minutes before.

Now I was her confessor and I, too, carried the burden of her double dishonesty, along with the knowledge that Ben Mendel was a villain of the first order. Agitation swelled in my gut and I swallowed several times and cleared my throat to try to calm it.

A blackbird screeched from a high limb above us. We both looked up, then again to each other.

"Does Samuel know what you have just told me? About Reb Ben Mendel?"

Marta dropped her head as she shook it. "No, he doesn't. No one does, except you." She wrapped her shawl around her shoulders and hunched down.

"How did this happen, Marta? When did it occur? Has it happened more than once?"

I was astounded by her confession. I saw the man's face: his dark mustache and beard that surrounded thick lips, his formidable nose and those uncommon blue eyes. I was powerless as his image taunted me like a nightmare from which I could not awaken. I could only imagine the burden that Marta bore.

Her voice came out small and weak. "At the first lesson… he told me that he would teach me if I didn't say anything to anyone about… "

She made a bad face, took a deep breath, and then began again. "Especially not to my mother. I told him yes, I would do that – because I wanted to learn to play the violin so much. But… I'm bad for saying yes." She looked up, finally, into my eyes again.

I hoped to encourage her to continue, but I had to blink to keep the tears from occluding my own vision.

"I know I'm bad. I'll never grow up to be a nice lady, or get married or have children."

I reached out and patted her arm, but she immediately shied away from my touch.

"Of course you will. Of course you'll grow up, Marta. You'll have a fine husband and many lovely children and you'll be good to them. Surely I know this much about you." At least, I hoped what I said was true.

When she looked off in thought, I saw – in her moment of reverie – the beautiful woman she would become. The child before me had regal bearing. She carried herself, even as a girl of nine, with grace and poise. I remembered when I first saw her on the hill in town, how even before I knew her there was something about her that drew my attention.

I supposed that, for a person who possessed the musical sensitivity and God-given gifts of Marta, the trials and sorrows of life might have an overwhelming effect. But, what about such an evil intrusion as had befallen her? What effect would that have on her?

She wiped her nose and face on a rag from her pocket, then looked at me with great despair. "I love that violin, Reb Thanhausser. I love to play it, I love to learn it, and I love to hear it. I love to look at it and I love the feel of it, too." Marta's hands moved through the air - they spoke with her.

"When I play music on my violin, a lighted tunnel to heaven opens up and then I'm with God. It's the most beautiful and peaceful place that anyone could ever imagine. I love it so much."

Her words surprised me as I, too, felt closer to God when she played the violin. She remained composed so I was silent.

"The music I hear when I play my violin, it speaks to me, right to my soul. It tells me that it's alright for me to be alive." She wrapped her arms around herself.

I was stunned. "But, of course it is alright for you

to be alive, Marta! You are as special in God's eyes as anyone… maybe you are even more special because of your gifts. Surely God cannot be unhappy with a child who makes such beautiful music in the world."

Could her terrible experiences truly produce such a hatred of herself as a result? How I wanted to reach out to her with a touch of comfort.

She folded her hands in her lap and spoke with certainty, "I am not special, Reb Thanhausser. I know that better than anyone. I am a terrible, ugly, person. I'm so ashamed… I should just go ahead and die!" With that, she grabbed her knees, pressed her forehead against them, and rocked fore and aft.

I was brought up short. Never had I heard a girl speak of herself with such bitterness. She spoke of her own death, her own ugliness and shame. Only someone whose thoughts dwelt among the most ill-disposed demons could say such things. And, Ben Mendel was, indeed, such a one.

A thunderbolt shot through me. If it was true that an apple did not fall far from the tree, then what kind of twisted result was Marta destined to become with Chanah Lindauer for a mother? She… who was once a happy, singing child herself, but later turned bitter and haughty – and was the tree from whence my sad, little Marta had fallen.

And, what, or should I say *who*, was the demon that

had sent Chanah down the path of enmity and ill will? I had watched the transformation of Marta with my own eyes, but was able only to speculate upon Chanah's earlier fall, or rather… push, from grace.

Several quiet moments passed before I was able to respond. Marta ran a finger through the pine needles and kept her head down. Misery rose off her like mist.

Across the clearing, a fawn and its mother ambled through, both alert to our presence. I would have made some motion to her so she could see them as well, but she did not welcome any touch from me, and my voice would surely have sent them off. When they disappeared into the woods, I gathered myself together.

The child had confessed to me in confidence. My solemn wish was to provide her with the devotion she sought and needed. I spoke quietly.

"My dear Marta." She looked up and I strove to connect my words to my heart. "For whatever travails you have endured until now, I am sorry for you." A small nod assured me that she understood the depth of my regret for her unfortunate situation. "The question now before us is how to proceed? We must tell your mother…"

"NO!" She jumped up and faced me with clenched fists. "You promised, Reb Thanhausser… you promised!"

Such a fierce little thing she was.

"But surely you understand that your mother must know. This man must not be allowed near you ever again. He must be prosecuted for his transgressions against you."

Marta's fervor erupted. "Would you have the violin taken from my hands? Would you have me punished, sir, and the violin cast away forever from my life?" She stomped a foot with each question. "... So that I may never again dwell among the angels with my music? Oh, it's too much... too much." She slumped to her knees.

"Why did you tell me then, Marta? What else is there to do but recount to your mother what you have endured these past months..."

Silent tears slid down her cheeks. "You promised... you promised."

Yes, I had promised her that I would not tell Madam Lindauer that she studied violin under the tutelage of Mordechai Ben Mendel. But I had not promised to withhold truths about such vile and dishonorable behavior as she described of the man. There was no doubt that he would be removed from the house and all musical instruction, Samuel's included, would cease.

It would mean the end of Marta's musical life. Even with the acknowledged consideration of the girl's demonstrated capacity, the antipathy that Chanah Lindauer bore toward her younger daughter would prevail and would mean even more hardship and unhappiness for her.

Could I knowingly set that woman upon the precious child who sat in a heap before me in the woods? Did I have any other option? I sought an answer to my quandary.

"Tell me this, Marta. Why did you reveal this to me about Reb Ben Mendel? Did you not think that I must profess the truth of what you have uttered to your mother?"

The whole of the predicament was made plain through Marta's response. She merely shrugged, forsaken and forlorn, hopeless as an old beggar.

We sat in that lovely clearing as the afternoon waned, both of us wretched and damned. Marta was ruined and had little or nothing to fashion hope upon, and I faced the most onerous decision of my life. The words of Isaiah came to me: *"Surely, God is my salvation; I will trust and not be afraid. The Lord is my strength and my song; He has become my salvation."*

Oh, were that I was a brave man. In that moment, I sent a prayer to the Holy One. I asked for help in my hour of need; for the patience and wisdom that would be required of me to guide this child to safety, to give me fortitude to help foster this most unfortunate of predicaments to a satisfactory conclusion.

I resolved that I was bound by my word not to speak to Madam Lindauer of the calamitous misery that had befallen her daughter, yet I was under no such promise concerning Ben Mendel. It was toward the fiend himself that I would direct my incredulity and outrage. What kind of man would exploit a child covertly – beneath the awareness of the authority of the house? Or, misuse a child period, under the guise of great mentor and tutor, or under any guise for that matter? Were there other innocents that had fallen prey to the *dybbuk's* depravity? I fervently hoped not.

And, what of Marta's fate? Before me sat a child who possessed rare gifts and abilities. A young girl who willingly traded the fulfillment of her passion for the ruination of her very body so that she might learn to play the music that brought her closer to God. And then required, nay *demanded,* that I remove myself as a barrier to her complicity and allow her to continue on this sordid path!

What kind of child did that? Only one whose very existence was compromised to the point of hopelessness, I feared, or one whose enflamed compulsion was determined to surmount any obstacle, whatever the cost.

"Marta, listen to me."

She untwisted her fist from her apron and looked

up.

"I will not tell your mother… not yet, anyway."

She brightened.

"But, I will speak with Reb Ben Mendel at my first opportunity, and will insist that he cease his inappropriate advances toward you."

My leverage would be to threaten to bring his heinous behavior to light. In addition, I would insist on my presence in the room whenever Marta was with him.

Of course, I didn't want to think of the problems posed for myself with such a proposition, or what it meant for my conscience and moral self to participate in the additional subterfuge required for Madam Lindauer's continued ignorance of the matter… *oy gevalt*.

Marta stood up and brushed pine needles off her skirts and apron.

"Then I can keep playing my violin and learning from Reb Ben Mendel? And you won't tell my mother?"

A twisted thing, like a knotted cord, coiled its way through my gut.

"I will do my best, Marta. That is all I can promise you."

She nearly smiled.

"But, the man should answer for his villainy and I

am not the one to administer his punishment. Do you understand? Justice should come from the town fathers, not me..."

She interrupted my last words. "But you promised, Reb Thanhausser. You *know* that if you tell those men, I'll lose my violin."

We stood together in the quiet glen.

"Yes, that's true. So, I'll speak first with Reb Ben Mendel." I hardened my voice. "But, if I must, I will seek the help of others in order to solve this dilemma."

Although she scowled at my pronouncement, it was short-lived. Marta wiped the end of her tears away and gave a small curtsy of thanks. She appeared relieved and for that, I offered up a silent prayer of gratitude. For now at least, some of her burden was lifted.

I took hold of her small hand for just a moment as she led us out of the grove, through the brambles and onto the path that would return us to the inn.

My thoughts reeled. The child experienced everything deeply and with such strong emotion. Already, at her young age, she was the most passionate person I had ever met.

As we entered the back gate, Marta silently headed off to her chores and I retrieved my apron and basket. I realized just then that I had never felt as intimately acquainted with another human soul as I had with young Marta during our time together in the woods.

God had placed her in my path for a reason. What was that reason?

CHAPTER 9

Autumn waned, and our lives resumed their usual routines. Samuel continued his twice-daily classes with me as the time for his *bar mitzvah* drew closer. He was scheduled to become officially accountable for his actions at his coming of age ceremony in the dark of winter, after *Chanukah,* on the *Shabbos* following his thirteenth birthday.

However, because his father died when he was young, and he was possessed of a godly character, Samuel had already stepped forth and proved his mettle as a member of the community to everyone in the village. His *bar mitzvah* would be but a formality to usher him into adulthood, into the brotherhood of Jews. His inquisitive nature and superb moral accuracy foretold of a *mensch.* He would be an upstanding citizen.

Jebenhausen was home to many such men. Nine of them had gone directly to the Barons von Liebenstein five years previous, and had secured the lands and protections that enabled us all to live with more security than our brethren who struggled endlessly for the opportunity to live un-assailed throughout Europe. I was proud to be a part of the Jebenhausen community and also pleased to help Samuel enter into our midst. With the new ways of thinking about Judaism and assimilation, it was imperative that he be prepared for the fresh ideas of the greater world.

Not all of the inhabitants of our thriving village embraced new ideas, however. I'm certain that conversations - such as the one that enlivened us at the Lindauer inn the very night of Marta's appalling disclosure - were being carried out all across Germany. The main topic was: man's basic human rights, a notion far removed from a Jew's experience. Most had difficulty imagining life out from under the heavy restrictions, taxes and insults that had plagued them and their fathers and grandfathers for longer than they could remember.

I was impressed with Samuel's contributions to the

exchange which took place that evening - a rainy, late autumn evening soaker - after Marta and Hindel had cleared away the meal dishes. On that particular night we were graced with the presence of Elias Gutmann, one of the respected founders of Jebenhausen and *parnas* - president of the congregation - who came by the inn on occasion for beer and newsworthy exchange.

There happened to be a family of four from Berlin ensconced at the inn that evening, as well, along with several men from town who had stopped by to share camaraderie and a brew.

Ben Mendel, who was often requested to share his music with other eager and appreciative audiences in the village and surrounding areas, was not present for dinner or yet when the conversation commenced after the meal.

My own repast went mostly untouched as I had agitation within that did not favor compliant digestion. I did not look forward to seeing the man. When I envisioned the prospect of a confrontation with him, my victuals turned unfriendly.

Gutmann surprised everyone in the room when he pulled a paper from his coat, unfolded it and began.

"Gentlemen and ladies, we have reached the point in the development of Jebenhausen wherein it is time to think about providing a new school and a bigger synagogue for our congregation."

The men in the room, as well as the woman from Berlin, nodded their heads. Chanah Lindauer picked at her teeth with a wood splinter near the fireplace but did not respond. She appeared wary, but then, she always appeared so.

Gutmann continued.

"I also believe it would be worthwhile for you to understand something of what has been going on in the greater world. I have done some reading of late concerning an Edict of Toleration that the Habsburg Monarchy in Austria put forth at the beginning of the Christian year." He opened the paper in his hand. "Here's what the prologue says, 'This policy paper aims at making the Jewish population useful to the state…' "

An old timer from town threw up his hands and interrupted.

"Of course that's what it says. What other reason would there be for granting Jews more privileges? God forbid it should be because of humanitarian reasons. No, it's so we can be useful to the state. Believe me… the reddest apple has a worm in it!"

Immediately, the young voice of Samuel interjected.

"Sir, a political body will only grant privileges to a group if it will be economically advantageous for them to do so. Few in history have granted anything to the Jews unless the Jews paid dearly for those rights. Here, in Jebenhausen, where we live in peace with our Christian neighbors, we are lucky to have the freedom of our religious life, but that is not the case elsewhere in Germany. Now, the Jews of Austria will have more freedom. This is good."

For a moment, no one in the room said a word. Elias Gutmann turned his body to look at Samuel, nodded his head, and finally spoke.

"Yes, Samuel, you are absolutely correct." Then, he turned back around.

"Please allow me to continue… The edict goes on to say that the Austrian plan is to make Jews useful to the Empire through better education and enlightenment of the Jewish youth, who should be directed to the sciences, the arts and the crafts. Of course, gentlemen," he paused and partook of a large swig of beer, wiped his arm across his beard, looked each man around the table in the eye, Samuel included, and then continued… "These improvements will aid the Jews more than they will aid Austria."

"And how is that?"

It was another old man, Moishe Weil, a respected Talmudic scholar in the village. "What possible good can come from, God forbid, an Austrian-speaking Jew who can recite all the laws of science before he can recite God's laws? What's wrong with the apprentice system we now have? We should keep our youth close…" His fist pounded on the table, "…among our own, not disperse them into the Christian world."

Weil was a teacher who had the answer for every question, biblical or otherwise, that was put to him by the men of Jebenhausen. His opinions carried much weight in people's minds.

I had a different perspective from Weil's, though. My station revealed to me that I was only a guide for my students, not their master. Each young man's future was his own choice; it was not for me to say which path he should follow. There was so much more in life that I did not know than what I did. I could only encourage the acquisition of knowledge and question the direction of my students' moral thoughts when integrity instructed me to do so.

Samuel jumped into the fray.

"I am a student, sir, and not yet even a *bar mitzvah*, but I do know that my prospects locally and in greater Germany will be bettered, not reduced, if I have an understanding of the German language and subjects of which the greater world knows much and I know little."

What a large mind resided in that small boy. I had been waiting for such a conversation so I might broach the subject of Samuel's German studies with his mother, although I did not look forward to the prospect. He made my argument toward his mother better than I could. I considered that it was entirely possible that he would make his way in God's creation as something other than an innkeeper.

Gutmann continued.

"We have decided that here in Jebenhausen, it will benefit us to build two schools for our children… a German school and a Jewish school. In the German school our children will learn reading and writing in German, and arithmetic…"

"In German, *kein ayin hora*!" Weil pounded another fist on the table.

"Yes, in German. But, they will also learn Hebrew in the Jewish school in preparation for *bar mitzvahs*." Gutmann ran his fingers through his beard. "I have drawn up a list of steps we must take. It's time we get serious about our progress as a forward-thinking village.

"We know what it means." … A fellow from town, the one with the tics. "It means, and may I not live to see the day, that our children will stop learning Yiddish and speak, instead, the language of the Germans… peh!"

When he leaned over and spat on the floor, Chanah cleared her throat and pointedly crossed her arms but the man paid no attention.

Elias Gutmann was a patient man. He had a voice that calmed, a manner that reassured.

"Remember, the Germans are our neighbors. They built the fine homes we are now living in. And yes, henceforth, our school books will be printed in German, and… we should all learn to speak the German language. However, if we talk to our little ones in Yiddish at home, as we do now, they will learn it as their first language."

He stopped and looked around at all present, then raised his arms. "In Austria, Jewish children may now attend state schools and universities. Is this not a wonderful thing?"

The Berliner held onto the lapels of his coat while he spoke. "Yes, this is so. And, listen gentlemen, someday soon, not only will our children attend universities, but we shall open factories and become merchants in trade with the greater world, and without having to pay such extortionate taxes and fees. German Jews will, someday, become first class citizens, with all the rights inherent in that designation."

He lifted his stein in a toast and others joined him. "To equality for the Jews!"

"And what will become of our Jewishness if we all stop speaking Yiddish and teaching it to our children?" A stooped old man from town stood up and supported his trembling body with his hands on the table. "Will we say our prayers in German rather than Hebrew? Will our children become Germans first and Jews second?"

Numerous voices grumbled assent. Gutmann spread his hands in the air to quiet everyone.

"I understand your concerns gentlemen. Of course our prayers will be said in Hebrew… of course. But, if we are to live peacefully among our German brethren, then I see no better way than to join their culture as speakers of the language. Assimilation is the answer that will help us move forward - peacefully and with full rights."

Chanah sat on her stool beside the hearth with her attention half on the fire and half on the conversation. I knew she listened closely even though it didn't appear so, as she offered a barely audible grunt at particular moments.

Hindel paid little attention to the exchange. She was more inclined to hover near the son of the Berlin couple who were in Jebenhausen for a meeting with a prospective husband for their daughter. When her face did not project its usual sourness, Hindel presented as a likely young woman, and the young man noticed her. She brought to mind a spider as she carefully and meticulously drew him in with her solicitous attention.

I saw that Madam Lindauer was aware of her daughter's behavior but allowed it to continue, and I could only surmise that, for Hindel to marry a man with such means, her mother would tolerate a great deal.

Elias Gutmann continued.

"The men from the council are moving forward with proposals for the new school. We will meet Tuesday next at my home, after mid-day *shul*, to draw up some plans." He turned toward me. "Thanhausser, we would like your input concerning these proposals. Your name has been mentioned as a potential hire for the school. Samuel's *bar mitzvah* comes in a few months, yes? At which time you will be seeking new employment, yes?"

This was news to me and welcome at that. I had spent some time in contemplation as to my next employment, with mixed thoughts concerning the Lindauer children.

How would Marta fare without the security that my confidence afforded her? I knew that she relied on my presence at the inn in order to soften the harsh conditions under which she labored. Our clandestine, sporadic conversations appeared to alleviate some of the darkness from her countenance, at least temporarily, and for that I was grateful to be present in her life. Now, with my new understanding of her situation, there was no clear path forward for me.

However, in the deep recesses of my soul, I longed to live again among those whose appreciation for God's gift of life brought gladness and lightness to living, as did my own parents' gratitude in the modest home of my childhood. The fractious prate and endless vituperation delivered by Madam Lindauer and her daughter rubbed me like an ill-fitted harness, as I know it did for Marta. Frankly, Elias Gutmann's offer was manna to me.

I nodded heartily at Gutmann. "Yes, sir. I am interested in learning more about the position. I think it may be a good fit for both of us."

I could tell that Samuel thought it was a good idea. He lifted his mug as though to make a toast.

"Gentlemen, you will not find a more suitable teacher for your school, I assure you. But, you mayn't have him until I am *bar mitzvah* and can join in a *minyan* with the rest of you." Then, he lifted his drink higher and shouted *l'chaim!* and we all drank to the future.

"So, you do teach German, then."

Madam Lindauer stood up with purpose and interrupted the happy moment. She crossed her arms and directed her dark, malevolent eyes at me. "And, does my son now know German?"

Of course, I felt like a naughty child and required several moments to gather myself and prepare a response. When I tried to speak, my voice broke like Samuel's. I cleared my throat and began again.

"Yes, Madam, I do and he does."

Brevity was my best option as there was an audience present - a silent, attentive audience. I returned her stare without malice and waited.

Chanah paced for a moment, obviously unsure of how to proceed. Was she going to rail at me with Elias Gutmann and the others seated in her dining room?

Samuel, ever the conciliator, joined me on his feet and spoke to his mother like a young curly-headed Solomon the Wise.

"Mother, I wanted to learn German. The fault lies completely with me. Do not think for a moment that this was Reb Thanhausser's doing." He looked at me with his thoughtful expression. "You should *thank* my teacher, for he has prepared me for success in the larger world…"

Chanah interrupted.

"What do I care of the larger world, Samuel? I have an inn to run - you are needed here and nowhere else." She wedged her hands into her hips and leaned toward him, squinted through one eye and cocked her head.

"Don't you be getting big ideas about the world Master Samuel. You are an innkeeper's son and you, too, shall become an innkeeper. Do you think I have enjoyed taking on all the work that your father should have been doing all these years? I have been waiting for the day when you are ready to assume some responsibility, and it is nearly here." Her pointer finger shot forward like a gun in time with her words. "If the work was good enough for your father and grandfather, it's good enough for you. The greater world... hah!"

The presentation left no room for a response. Samuel, in his sagacity, merely nodded respectfully toward his mother, made a shallow bow to me and then sat down. His expression remained composed, but I knew the lad - he had ideas, that one. No doubt we would have conversation at a later time.

The strong voice of Elias Gutmann broke the awkward silence of the room.

"Thank you for your recommendation, Samuel. I have had numerous conversations with Ascher Thanhausser," Here he tipped his hat toward me, "And have found him to be in possession of a fine character and nimble mind. The timing of our need for his services should coincide perfectly with the construction of the school."

Gutmann and the others went back and forth for another quarter hour. Chanah Lindauer sent Marta to work behind one of the counters with a bucket and brush. The wiles of Hindel kept the younger Berliner occupied as his sister and mother listened into the conversation or bent their heads together in private natter.

My own inclination was, as always, to observe, listen with care and say little. Madam Lindauer reserved further comment to me, but I knew that I would hear from her soon enough.

As the evening neared its close, Mordechai Ben Mendel returned to the inn. He surveyed the gathering from the doorway, shook rainwater from the shoulders of his cloak, reached beneath the wrap and pulled out the precious black violin case. When he looked up, our eyes met for the briefest of moments and my heart hammered. I noticed, in his haughty stance and curled lip, a different man from the one I had perceived before. A chill arced through me. Who was this Mordechai Ben Mendel, this man who was Marta's teacher? With so many people in the room, it was not the time for me to confront him. I would have to wait for a more advantageous opportunity.

When he entered the dining room to pay his respects to those present, the usual unanimous requests for his violin music rose from the group. I shot a concealed glance in Marta's direction, but saw only the bottoms of her boots as she scrubbed behind the counter.

Samuel caught my eye with a raised eyebrow, but of course I responded not at all. Marta's secrets lived every moment among us and floated through our lives like a wraith. However, even Samuel was unaware of Marta's latest confession - a much more heinous concealment than he knew.

The master opened his case on a table, rosined the bow, lifted the instrument to his shoulder, and began to play. It was difficult to reconcile the remarkable sounds we heard with the man whom Marta had described to me. How could beautiful music like that come forth from such a fiend?

The burden of my illicit knowledge, like a boulder's weight, produced within me a hot core of unease. I looked around, but all attention was on Ben Mendel and I was grateful, in that crowded room, for the diversion that the musician provided. Had he not performed just then, I fear I may not have had the self-control to regulate my own behavior. As it was, I used great restraint to avoid a confrontation propelled by anger. Marta's cause would be best served if my actions and protestations remained in control, rather than if I were to allow an altercation to interrupt the smooth flow of the evening and produce disquiet among the group. I vowed to seek out Ben Mendel after the inhabitants of the inn dispersed for the night.

At the end of Ben Mendel's performance, several requests were made of Samuel to take a turn on the violin, which he did with aplomb. However, his music did not compare with the accuracy and liveliness of Marta's, nor did he produced the depth of feeling that she managed to convey each time I heard her. The girl remained behind the counter, hidden from view, while Samuel performed.

Madam Lindauer watched and listened to Samuel, her arms folded in approval, her normally cheerless countenance augmented to a less severe expression. I detected pride in her stance although it was minimally displayed. Samuel was indeed a worthy son, with a fine start on the violin.

As he played, I watched those present in the room. Hindel served a beer to Mordechai Ben Mendel while he observed Samuel's playing. In the company of others, the man appeared to be cheerful and of good character. Until that day, although I could not say that I liked him, I had thought well enough of him and enjoyed his music. How different he looked to me just then - like a brigand, a man whose evil side lurked beneath the surface. His eyes shifted around the room and for one brief uncomfortable moment hooked into mine.

Had I not been seated I might have staggered from the strength of his gaze, but I did not intend to allow a rogue to get the better of me. I returned his look with the surety of the conviction that grew within me - that the man's monstrous actions would be brought to light and he would be punished for them. Then, I finished my beer for fortification.

The townsmen, Gutmann and Weil included, watched and listened spellbound to Samuel's performance. As pleasantly as he played, I wished that there might be an opportunity for Marta to share her gifts with her mother and the rest of the company at the inn. If they would hear her but once, they would understand why the child had sought to learn, even under such ghastly conditions. Alas, I was a hopeless dreamer where Marta was concerned.

Across the room, the wife of the Berliner appeared fraught with agitation. She persisted with loud rude whispers to her husband throughout Samuel's presentation as she had during Ben Mendel's. I had met other city dwellers in my travels but had never observed such *chutzpah* from an urbanite. I noticed that several others in the room were also not well pleased by the woman's conduct. But, Chanah Lindauer's attention remained affixed on Samuel. She appeared unconcerned with the woman's display of bad manners.

When Samuel finished his final melody he bowed to applause all around. Mordechai Ben Mendel, hailed as hero for his fine work as Samuel's teacher, accepted accolades from the group. Then, he gathered his violin, the beautiful instrument that bound us in subterfuge, made his goodbyes for the evening and departed up the stairs to his room.

The man's exit signaled day's end. Immediately the room filled with the scrapes of chairs and benches as the men from town stood and prepared to leave. The Berlin family rose, as well. I had just moments not only to collect my thoughts, but also to summon my bravery.

Never had I faced such an odious task. Mordechai Ben Mendel was a man who carried his secrets well - his wicked loathsome nature and his despicable behaviors. The more I thought on it, the angrier I felt.

Just as I was about to chase the blackguard up the stairs, a fracas broke out right there in the room. The Berliner had his wife by an arm, but she twisted and shrieked, distraught beyond control.

"It's him! I'm telling you, Chaim. He's one and the same!" The woman was vehement. She spat the words toward her husband, "If you don't say something immediately, I will!"

She gave a final heave of her arm away from her husband's grasp and gathered her shawl around her shoulders in an attempt to settle herself. Then, she lurched toward Chanah. "Do you know who that man is? The one who plays the violin and teaches your son?"

Her husband bared his teeth in mortification. "Mrs.

Rohrbacher! Control yourself."

He reached out once more, clasped her upper arm and drew her back to his side. Then he whispered loudly in her ear, loud enough for everyone present to hear. "Now is not the time. Wait until present company has left – then you may speak privately with Madam Lindauer."

Chanah Lindauer squinted her eyes at Madam Rohrbacher.

"What? What is it about Ben Mendel that you can't wait to tell me?"

I could hardly believe it. Madam Lindauer mocked the woman. Their respective allotment of *chutzpah* appeared evenly matched. My own flesh went wobbly and my strength began to falter. I quailed as I stood there, too distressed to move. How could Mrs. Rohrbacher know about Ben Mendel? More… was it the moment for me to confront the devil?

Elias Gutmann stepped forward with his hands in the air to help mollify the commotion.

"Let us hear what Mrs. Rohrbacher has to say. There is obviously something quite serious troubling her." Several heads nodded agreement.

He turned toward the nervous woman. "Madam, please explain to us what is upsetting you so."

Samuel moved quickly to stand by my side and I must admit, I appreciated the gesture. Hindel took root where she stood beside her mother, her face a mix of scorn and wonder. She appeared to enjoy the discomfiture of those around her.

From my position, I was unable to see Marta at all, busied as she was behind the counter. And, rather than rush away from the drama at hand to confront Ben Mendel, I decided to wait in order to hear Mrs. Rohrbacher's disclosure. All stood and listened keenly as she spoke.

"That man, your Reb Ben Mendel," she gestured with her head toward the stairway, "is a base and dishonorable person. He is a perpetrator of dastardly deeds."

A sharp, collective intake of breath coursed through the room. My own astonishment was not because of her news but because she, too, appeared to know what I did about the man.

Chanah maintained her wary look: one hand perched on a hip in her usual defiant stance. When she spoke her voice held a threat.

"Be careful what you say here, Madam. This is my home. I don't appreciate trouble in this inn."

Mrs. Rohrbacher peered down her nose at Chanah.

"I should think you would *want* to know if someone was harming your children, yes?"

There ceased to be enough air in the room. With so many gathered in close, I found I could not take a full breath. I took one step back and saw Marta as she stood apart from the others behind the counter. A pale halo of clouded red light surrounded her like an aura. The child's face was fixed - her mouth made a tight line. Those eyes burned into mine, pleaded for deliverance, but I could do nothing.

Tension twined through the room. Then, the Berliner spoke.

"My wife has information about the violin master that she feels is important for you to know, Madam Lindauer. However, I'm not certain that everyone present needs to know, as well." He gestured to the group around him.

Chanah flipped her hand up from the wrist with a dismissive motion.

"Go ahead. Say what you have to say. It's half said already."

I had seen her haughtiness before, but to be arrogant at such a moment - well, *Gott im Himmel,* what was going to happen?

Air or no air, I could not have breathed just then, even if paradise had opened its doors and bade me welcome. I fixed my uncertain gaze on Marta and awaited Armageddon.

Mrs. Rohrbacher did not hesitate further.

"I know of the man… from Berlin… he was a teacher there, a teacher of the violin to a friend's daughter… a close friend."

A magnificent flash of lightning lit the room with ghoulish daylight followed in the next instant by a loud crash and thunderous roll. A *schreck* bowled through me. Then, rain snapped against the shuttered windows and the woman continued.

"That Ben Mendel, he taught the child to play the violin, yes he did. But, he also preyed on that young girl… his student." She looked around and then lowered her voice. "He, he… defiled her!"

Samuel looked at me, his startled eyes shocked with new understanding. I returned his look with a curt nod of confirmation.

Chanah Lindauer appeared less concerned. She spoke slowly, with some caution.

"Ben Mendel teaches my son, not my daughters. There's nothing to worry about here." Then she turned to Samuel. "Isn't that correct, Samuel?"

Samuel answered carefully. "Yes, mother. The man has never laid a finger on me." But, I saw in his response, fear and disquiet for his little sister's welfare, although he did not look in Marta's direction.

For several long moments, there was not any movement or response from the group. Then, Elias Gutmann shifted into action.

"Madam Rohrbacher? You have made a grave accusation against Mordechai Ben Mendel. From what we here in Jebenhausen know of the man, there have been no transgressions by him against any young girls."

I moved only my eyes in order to avoid drawing attention to myself, but I sought to find Marta, who stood - like a specter - back away from the others. I had only an instant to reflect upon my astonishment of her having told me on that very day of her collusion with the fiend, of the price she paid daily in order to realize her musical passion. She looked hollow, like a small, empty husk. There were no tears, no hysterical demonstrations. Instead, she appeared defeated and ready to accept whatever horror destiny threw her way.

The Berliner added his perspective.

"Gentlemen, ladies, you would be wise to question Ben Mendel. He appears to be the very same scoundrel who was run out of Berlin last spring. I don't know how he made his way to Jebenhausen, but he is here, in this house, now!"

Gutmann pointed to me, and then to another.

"Thanhausser… Weil… Follow me. We'll bring the man downstairs for interrogation… immediately!"

We left the gawking crowd and made our way upstairs to Ben Mendel's room. He appeared surprised and exempted his participation due to fatigue and a headache. A more despicable man I had never had the displeasure of knowing. In his inimitable way, Gutmann convinced the rogue that he had no choice other than to descend the stairs and have it out.

"Ben Mendel, you can speak with us now or we can call upon the constable and have him detain you for further questioning. No one from Jebenhausen has accused you of anything. It may be that this woman has mistaken your identity and you have nothing to fear. In any case, you do not have a hostile audience here at the inn as you will if you're turned over to a higher authority."

Mordechai Ben Mendel paled as he stood there in the lantern light. The dark hollows of his eyes and cheeks deepened in contrast to the sallow clammy pallor of his skin. Those blue eyes sharpened their scrutiny and glinted at the three of us who stood before him.

"You have nothing on me." He sneered. "Talk to Samuel… I never touched him." He darted looks around the hallway and dots of perspiration shimmered on his forehead.

Gutmann took ahold of the man's arm and maneuvered him toward the stairs.

"We spoke with Samuel and he corroborated what you are saying. It's the Rohrbachers' claim that we wish to address."

CHAPTER 10

The room quieted when Madam Rohrbacher stepped over and stood before Ben Mendel. As she looked at him, her face frowned and hardened. She turned toward her husband and nodded once, sharply.

The culprit focused his eyes on no one but held his body rigid. Although he was not tied to the chair, the men in the room bristled and moved around until we stood and faced him in a tight ring with Chanah, Hindel, the Rohrbacher daughter and Marta behind us. The circle then closed in further until Madam Rohrbacher was squeezed back out of the *minyan*, also.

We formed a barrier in front of Ben Mendel.

The room was darkened with the night, but the candlelight from several hands reflected off the nervous sheen on his face and neck… a macabre apparition.

Never in all my days had I been witness to such a scene. To be the one person in the room, other than Marta, who knew the real truth about Mordechai Ben Mendel, was not a station that I was happy to hold. In those moments before Elias Gutmann began his interrogation, my heart pounded a wild tattoo and my knees trembled and weakened.

What Marta must have felt, well I abandoned that awful thought and turned my attention toward the inner circle. Gutmann cleared his throat and began.

"Mordechai Ben Mendel – do you recognize this woman, Madam Rohrbacher?"

The fiend's eyes flashed and a sneer twisted his mouth into a wicked grimace. He looked directly at her and then, to my surprise, in a calm and controlled voice, he answered.

"No, I have never seen her before in my life."

Madam Rohrbacher's voice broke in. "Oh yes he has!"

Everyone turned to look at her – her neck and face reddened, her agitation was pronounced. Then, we men moved back into place before Ben Mendel.

Gutmann's response came immediately.

"But, you are aware of the accusation she has made against you?"

Ben Mendel paused. The man had self-control, and it occurred to me that, as an accomplished musician and performer, his ability to present a calm façade was probably well honed. I'm certain that I did not breathe.

"I have not harmed my student Samuel in any way."

He turned his unpleasant gaze toward the boy, who stood in solidarity with the men before the accused. All eyes moved as one to peer at Samuel. Again, with his mouth drawn tight, Samuel gave a brief, affirmative nod, and then he flicked a quick glance in my direction. *Gott im Himmel,* what next?

Gutmann crossed his arms and leaned toward Ben Mendel. He began to speak but his voice failed, so he cleared his throat, rearranged his coat on his shoulders, and began again.

"Madam Rohrbacher tells us that you were run out of Berlin because of… because of… *indiscretions* with a young girl. Is this true?"

The man's directness sent a saber of fear through me. I did not want the moment to continue, yet I did not want it to stop. I wanted to help Marta, stand near her, protect her in any way that I might. But I was held, transfixed, by the appalling episode that was unfolding before me. The sober faces of the men in the group presaged imminent catastrophe and I knew that they were correct.

Ben Mendel squinted one eye shut and peered up at Elias Gutmann with the other but he refused to speak. Then he hawked a glob onto the floor directly in front of Gutmann and set his mouth into a hard line.

Elias Gutmann was a learned man. He had negotiated with a King. He knew what to say next.

"If you do not answer me, Ben Mendel, your guilt will be assumed. Did you defile that young girl in Berlin?"

Visceral hatred was an unfamiliar feeling to me. But, in that moment, I truly hated Mordechai Ben Mendel. I knew what he had done to my beautiful Marta in the sanctity of the child's own home. But, the man dug in. His obdurate stare did not waver. A slight tremble appeared in his fingers, the muscle in his jaw flexed, but that was all.

The room gasped in unison, yet his gaze remained locked with Gutmann's, like a taunt. As had happened repeatedly in that inn, I found no air to breathe, again with no way to exit from a horrendous situation. My feet were stuck where they stood, and my heartbeat was so loud and percussive that, for a moment, I heard only the roar inside my own head. I was thankful when Moishe Weil finally broke in.

"*Oy gevalt*!" The old man threw his hands up. "We have a criminal here!" He looked around at the men. "What should we do with him?"

Everyone burst forth with his own opinion of what to do until, amidst the clamor it became impossible to hear any one voice. I took a moment during the chaos to turn my head toward Marta.

She looked stricken. Her skin was blanched to the color of dust. Next to her, Hindel leaned over and whispered something in her ear, and Marta's eyes grew huge. Her hands rose and covered her mouth. She shook her head wildly at her sister, but Hindel crossed her arms in exact duplication of her mother's behavior, strode over to Elias Gutmann and, while she kept her eye on Marta, said something directly into his ear. I could not make it out because the chamber was filled with loud voices. Then, Gutmann raised his arms and called the room to order.

"Alright, alright. There are several options for what our next step should be. But, before we discuss them, Hindel would like to say something. Go ahead, Hindel."

I feared what she was going to do. I feared she was prepared to turn Marta in right along with Ben Mendel. In the moments before she spoke, Samuel disengaged from the men and walked over to his little sister. He faced the group defiantly with his body close to hers. Then he put his arm around her shoulder and pulled her closer. Marta looked dazed, and then Hindel did it. Her voice took on that superior tone. She appeared pleased with herself.

"I suggest, gentlemen, that you ask Marta what she knows about Reb Ben Mendel. She is a lying little sneak, aren't you Marta?"

Chanah Lindauer interrupted.

"What is this, Hindel? What are you talking about?"

No one moved or made a sound. Ben Mendel squirmed about in the chair, and Marta's entire body reflected dread. She slumped against Samuel. He shored her up with his arm before Hindel let loose.

"Listen, Mother… all of you. Your wonderful Marta has been keeping a big secret… haven't you, Marta dear?" She smeared the words with contempt.

How a girl could turn on her own sister, I could not fathom. Yet, because it was Hindel, it made sense. Only Madam Lindauer responded - everyone else remained silent, including Ben Mendel. But, all listened… rapt.

"What secret is this? What do you know, Samuel?"

The lad was made of gold, of that I am certain.

"Mother, gentlemen, guests… Marta is a special person. She has defied your rules, Mother… yes. But, that is because she has a talent that is beyond measure, and the passion to accompany that talent. If you would but listen to her you would understand."

Chanah walked over to Marta and Samuel, folded her arms in her usual haughty stance and raised her chin. Her voice was hard.

"What are you telling me? That Marta has learned to play the violin? Against my orders? Against natural law?" The tenor of her speech rose in volume and fury with each word. "Answer me! You little *zoyne*!"

As her mother had just called her a whore, Marta hung her head, but Samuel stood erect, his eyes set on his mother's, his arm securely around Marta's shoulder. In the room not a soul breathed. This was spectacle of the most lurid variety, and even I was gripped. Marta could not talk so Samuel responded.

"I'm telling you, Mother. She has a gift. She is..."

Chanah tore her arm down through the air like an axe.

"*Shah*! You dare to tell me that this girl has been playing the violin directly under my nose and no one told me?" Then, she wheeled around and pointed a finger at Mordechai Ben Mendel. "What kind of *goylem* are you? How dare you come into my home and abuse my generosity!"

A moment ticked by. Her eyes widened and then narrowed. She whispered hoarsely, "Have you defiled my own daughter, too? Are you as horrible a monster as this woman claims?"

Ben Mendel remained silent. He looked at no one. Chanah turned in a circle and eyeballed everyone in the room with a scathing look. Madam Rohrbacher held a hand over her heart and leaned away from her. The townsmen, including Weil, Gutmann and the Berliner, were aghast, some with their jaws wide open in stunned astonishment. Tension shackled the group. Outside, the rain and wind swirled around us - we petty and fallible human beings.

Marta's eyes rolled back until I saw only the whites, then she dropped in a heap toward the floor. Samuel eased her down and when she lay there, he stood and turned toward his mother.

"You will not accuse my sister of wrong-doing." A hiss arced through the room. "She has done only what God insisted that she do. You must direct your wrath toward the true villain here…" He pointed at Ben Mendel. "…*that* man."

Chaos, once again, engulfed the dining room. Two men took ahold of Ben Mendel's arms and held him down on the chair. The release brought about by Samuel's admission sent all present into a frenzied chaos. In the bedlam, I saw Samuel rush from the room via the back doorway, but it appeared that no one else noticed.

Madam Lindauer made no move to rescue or

rehabilitate Marta, who lay on the floor like a sleeping dog. I stepped over and stood beside her in order to protect her small body from those who milled about the room. Finally, Elias Gutmann, in his wisdom, sought to calm.

"Ladies, gentlemen. Let us have some order here… please." When the room quieted, he turned toward Chanah.

"Madam Lindauer, we are sorry for your troubles. I will personally speak to the women in the village so that they might offer their help and support in your time of need." He looked down at Marta. "Can someone aid this child? It appears she has fainted."

Chanah Lindauer's chest visibly heaved with distress, and Hindel's self-satisfied smirk provoked my own rage to the point that I used every bit of personal restraint I could muster to avoid throttling the shrew.

How ironic it was to me that the truly wicked one was not Marta, on whose life would be exacted a huge penalty, and whose only sin was that she bore the burden of her own passion. But wicked, indeed, was her sister, Hindel – the shameless inciter who saw herself as the heroine but possessed instead, the most contemptible sort of character.

It was Madam Rohrbacher who finally knelt down beside the girl. She placed a hand on Marta's forehead and then sought help from her son, who gathered the limp child and carried her from the room and up the stairs.

After further discussion, it was decided that Mordechai Ben Mendel would be taken to the livery where he would be locked in chains until his disposition could be determined. The constable was sent for. Nearly a quarter hour passed before he arrived, and I hoped against hope that my own culpability might go undetected. Alas, it was not to be.

While the men debated among themselves, I kept my head low. It was not long before Madam Lindauer pulled me aside. I knew I was found out, but that knowledge did not help my heart to remain calm. Her manner was accusatory and bold.

"Reb Thanhausser. What did you know about this?"

Although I towered over her, I felt small and powerless.

"I knew, Madam. I did. But, I was sworn to secrecy by the children."

It was the truth, but not a happy answer for me. I saw, immediately, the flash in her eyes… I was finished. No more *bar mitzvah* preparation for Samuel, no more glorious music or camaraderie from Samuel and that wonderful little girl.

"You pack your things and leave this very night."

With that, Chanah Lindauer turned her back on me and was done.

I left the dining room and climbed the stairs. Madam Rohrbacher sat on a chair beside Marta's bed and adjusted a damp cloth on the child's forehead. Marta was still – her paleness matched by the muslin sheet beneath her. The woman was kind, her voice was quiet. She looked up at me as I stood in the doorway.

"Pitiable child. She's had a terrible blow. I can't imagine why she would have gone against her mother's wishes like that." She fussed with Marta's hair and then smoothed the girl's skirts. "She'll recover, poor thing."

I hunched my shoulders up, then down. I would not speak for Marta. Her story, which I would always carry within my heart, was complex… tangled far beyond what would have been fitting to share with Madam Rohrbacher, or anyone for that matter.

After I stowed my few belongings into my pack, I went to Samuel's room to bid him farewell. The door was open but Samuel was not inside. I made my final descent from the familiar hallway and stood before the front door on the landing so that I might try to see the lad once more.

I looked into the meeting room where someone had tied Ben Mendel's wrists behind the chair. He sat with his eyes closed, his chin against his chest. What misery… what wretchedness accompanies some lives.

The longer I stood there, the stronger was my desire to go away from that place. Marta's fate was sealed beyond anything I could do to amend it, and Samuel and I, as men of the community, would not be strangers.

I thought about where I might stay on such a cold, blustery night, and then remembered Gutmann's earlier offer of a position with the new school. As I wished to remain in Jebenhausen for that, I felt sure that one of the other inns in town would have space for me. I had a few shekels in my pocket and heaviness in my heart… a rather inauspicious way to venture forth. I knew it would not take me long to relocate. But what, God forbid, would become of Marta?

I was surprised when I surveyed the disorder in the room and found no sign of Samuel. What made the most sense to me then, was to leave - to slip out unnoticed. I wanted no further part of the Ben Mendel dilemma and frankly, was glad to depart from the inn of iniquity as well.

At that moment, when I understood the void that would be left in my life without the light of Marta's daily presence, I was seized by a cold shudder. My heart clenched, dropped a beat, and turned over in my breast. I pounded my chest to set it right again and took a deep breath. I had borne grave loss before and would, I hoped, persevere.

When I opened the door a wave of cold wind and rain splattered against me. I tucked my head and struggled with the gate latch. Just as I stepped beyond the fence, Samuel staggered around the side of the inn and stumbled his way to the front door. In my dispirited state, it did not occur to me to question why he was out there. I called to him.

"Samuel!"

He lifted his head and I saw that he was completely drenched. His teeth chattered, his body shivered. Then he keeled over, lost his footing, slipped off the flagstone and landed sprawled in the mud. When I bent to lift him, he sobbed and grabbed my lapel.

"Don't tell, Reb Thanhausser. Don't tell them that you saw me out here... ever!"

"Of course, Samuel. Of course." I would have said anything to appease his anguish. "Let me help you..."

The boy held on as I hoisted him up. I knew that I did not want to go back into the inn, so I looked into his mournful eye.

"I have to leave now, but I'll see you at *shul*. Are you going to be alright?"

"What can be alright, now? Poor Marta. Poor, poor Marta."

Then, he opened the front door and half lurched, half fell inside. I turned away, pulled my coat around myself, and tromped down the hill.

If God had put me in Marta's life for a reason, as I earlier believed, or if she had been put into mine in order to complete some divine plan, well, the why of it all eluded me just then. Uncertainty was my only companion.

In three days' time, the village of Jebenhausen reeled with the terrible news of Samuel's sudden, untimely death due to exposure, and what I was certain was a broken heart. The town's shared grief was immediate and extreme. I mourned the boy deeply and made one visit to the inn to sit *shiva*, but, although I watched for her, Marta was nowhere in sight. I paid my respects, but I did not like being there.

Word also spread that Ben Mendel's beautiful violin went missing during that fateful night at the inn. Was there a connection between Samuel's foray out into the storm and the vanished violin? If so, he took the secret of its whereabouts with him to his grave.

The miscreant himself was carted off to Berlin to face charges there, along with a representative to plead Chanah Lindauer's case. Or should I say, Marta's.

Marta recovered, I heard. But, in the months following, as my position with the school developed, I kept to myself. And aside from a few sporadic glimpses of the furtive girl in the village, I had no further contact with her. Nor did I wish to set foot ever again in the Lindauer inn.

Part III

My Diary

A SMALL LIFE

by

Marta Lindauer

Age 16 years, 5 months

Jebenhausen, Germany

8 Tamuz, 5549

July 2, 1789

Paper ~ Pen ~ Ink ~ Candlelight

I haven't felt this way for such a long, long time... I'm filled with hope and shiny happiness. Can you see that wet spot on the page? That's my tear! Mine! Marta Lindauer, who never cries... never!

I made a discovery, in a bottom drawer, of the most exquisite quill, the most beautiful full inkbottle, and best of all, the most wonderful paper ever made in the entire world! There are two dozen large sheets and I intend to fill all of them, front and back, with as many words from my deepest soul as I can fit on them.

Now I can write about my life, my wishes, my dreams... if that's possible. Who should I write to? I'll write to an imaginary someone, the best friend anyone could ever have. Her name is Fraynd.

Dear Fraynd – I promise to be honest and true and, in return, you will listen silently to everything I have to say and not judge me and not make me feel stupid and like a waste of a person. I must be thrifty with my words. I have only a few pages to fill.

I measured and cut the beautiful blank pages with my shears and then, with a needle and thread, bound my own booklet. I pushed that needle through all those pages. Delirious joy! I doubled over and cried – all because of some paper and a pen.

Next, I put my booklet in the bottom of my basket and went out to the market for a few things. It felt good just to carry it around with me. On my way home, I visited the old weaver where I love to listen to the rhythmic clacking of his loom and laugh at his silly jokes. Yarn hanks hang in bunches on his walls and oh the colors! Reb Veberke is always happy to see me. Maybe he's the only person in Jebenhausen who is.

He stopped his work and unrolled a tapestry he had made. It was too large and awkward to hold so he draped it over the loom near the window. It was a beautiful sight to behold – a picture woven of yarns – blue mountains that looked far away, with clouds of yellow and purple and a pink sky, trees with many colored leaves and a silver river flowing toward the foreground.

The yarns made the surface bumpy and uneven – soft and scratchy. I wanted to pet his weaving like a cat and stare at it until the light was gone.

Finally, he rolled it back up and put it away. I told him it was wonderful because it was, and then I asked him why he had made it. He looked right into my eyes and whispered – even though I was alone with him – 'I use my God-given gifts to make something more lovely than bed sheets.' He winked at me. 'Don't get me wrong... I make excellent bed sheets.' His words thrilled me.

Then, I carefully pulled my booklet out of my basket and showed it to him. Here's what he said to me: 'Marta, here is your opportunity to tell your story – without anyone else's interference. And, Gott im Himmel, we do know that you have a story to tell.'

His voice is always so kind... he almost made me cry. I had to get out of there fast. After I thanked him, I left for home.

For so long I have wanted to write something that matters. When I can get away with it, I claim a scrap of paper to doodle on. I've made drawings with pieces of charcoal from the fireplace and colored them with berry juice. But, I've never had real paper of my own to use before. Now I can write down the stories that swirl through my thoughts all the time. This is a special day.

Thanks to the forgetful scribe who left me a treasure in the drawer, and with the encouragement of Reb Veberke, I plan to write in my little book until it bursts from the weight of so many words. Oh happy night...

10 Tamuz, 5549
July 4, 1789

MY BEGINNINGS

I will write the story of myself in as true a fashion as I am able and we'll see where that takes me...

The first person in my family to die since I was born was my father – David Lindauer. He had a horrible death. He was 26 years old. I was a baby but I've heard this story many times.

We all lived in a house with my mother's parents near the home of my father's parents in Freudental, a village close to Stuttgart. This was before we came to Jebenhausen. David and Chanah Lindauer and her parents Zayde and Bubby and the children: Hindel, Samuel and Marta (me). I think there was another girl born in there somewhere but no one talks about her. Bubby my grandmother said something once about that poor misshapen little thing but that's all I ever heard.

First my grandfather Zayde died – before I was born. He was old and it was expected. Then when I was only one year old – the story goes – my father, an innkeeper, was ambushed on a road by some bandits who stole his money and hit him on the head with a heavy stone.

They found him beside the road and carried him unconscious and bloody to the inn then laid him out on the table where he expired amid horrific grief and wailing by my mother, Hindel and Samuel and others who had crowded into the room.

I remember only one moment of that time. I was set out of the way in the wood box by the fireplace which was nearly empty of logs. At the same moment that a drip of cholent boiled over the edge of the kettle, hissed in the fire and sent a blast of smelly burnt soup at me – someone lifted a lantern over my father whose chest and entire upper body rose up just then in a violent crooked spasm. Then he seized and fell back down lifeless to the table.

I was suffocated by fear, clenched so tight I was unable to breathe in or out – when a sliver of wood got stuck in my hand - but there was no one to help me – all was terrible moans and weeping – and to this day I cannot eat anything that has been singed black in the fire – can't even stand the smell of it.

That's what I remember from when my father died. I also remember when he used to hold me high over his head and shake me up and around until I giggled and laughed. Then he would laugh, too. I can't remember what his face looked like but I remember that he loved me. Or it felt like he did.

We left my father's parents behind and moved to Jebenhausen when I was five years old in a cart packed with our table, big rolls of bedding and clothes and our kettles and dishes. I sat on top next to my old Bubby and had Sarah my doll to talk to and help me be brave on the journey because my sister Hindel, who is six years older, was not what I would call my friend. I will write more about her later.

Uncle Meyer, my father's brother, walked beside the horse and helped us move but he didn't stay with us after that. I think he went east so my mother had to run the new inn by herself.

It's a big house... we have an indoor and outdoor kitchen and 2 rooms on the ground floor, 4 rooms on the first, and 3 rooms on the second. At the far end of the back yard is the privy and on the other side of the house, near our outdoor kitchen and the shed, is our garden.

Hindel and I used to share a room on the second floor next to Samuel's room. He was our brother. I haven't written about Samuel because it makes me too sad. But I will try to write about him later, too.

Now I have my own garret room at the very top of our house. There's a tiny window that overlooks the garden and beyond that I can see the meadow and beyond that the forests, fields and Hohenstaufen mountain. When I need to be alone away from everything and everyone else, I run up here, open the shutters on my little window and look far out over the land.

If I sit completely still the birds will sing to me and I sing back to them – the melody of Bach that I used to play on my violin. I still know it even though I learned it seven years ago – when we had two teachers staying at the inn.

And I can only say that there is a story to tell concerning all that but I would rather not. I will write only about my brother's teacher, Reb Thanhausser. As for the other – he left his mess behind and I am that mess.

13 Tamuz, 5549
July 7, 1789

The teacher I wish to describe was named Reb Asher Thanhausser. He was the one who made the garden so nice. There are a lot of things I can write about him.

I catch a glimpse of him from time to time in town but I talk with almost no one beyond what is necessary to carry on the daily business of running the inn. I haven't had anything to do with him since Samuel died.

As for the Bach music and the other teacher, it won't be easy for me to write about that. But if I'm going to write honestly then I suppose I'll have to tell what happened and what I did that ruined my life. I miss my violin until my heart aches every single day but who cares about it anyway? It was a long time ago... no one cares any more. Not that they did then either.

My job when I was little was emptying chamber pots and helping in the kitchen when I wasn't cleaning something else. I was also in charge of making sure all the guests had water in their pitchers before they went to bed at night. I went up and down those stairs so many times – I still do.

For a while before my brother died I took over most of Hindel's chores. Now I do everything at the inn... I run it. My mother is no longer in a condition to do anything - she almost never goes upstairs anyway. More about her later, too.

It's a lot of work for me but I prefer to stay busy. If I don't I go down down down... to the heavy dark place where evil thoughts grow inside me like black mold.

The outward life I live here in the Lindauer inn

in Jebenhausen is not a true portrayal of what goes on inside me. My real life takes place behind dark doors, down in the shadowy and wicked depths of my soul. It's where these very words are coming up from.

If I hadn't found this paper, quill and ink I would surely have exploded eventually from the sheer burden of trying to live alone with myself for so long. At least if I write I have someone to talk to, even if imaginary, instead of mulling on my ugly thoughts until they rise up like challah dough and overtake me.

Some information about my mother: she sits at the table or in her spot beside the hearth and tells me what to do all day long as if I have no idea of what I'm doing. She also complains about how I'm doing things like the cooking or cleaning – which is what I do most of the time – and then complains afterwards of how I've ruined the dinner or how many crumbs are left in the corner after I've swept.

Bound by the rules of life, a mother is the one you cannot leave, cannot cross, and cannot help but love. Yet she thinks not of me, her daughter, but only of herself and her small hateful life. She preens like a queen who awaits her subjects and the entire world must bow before her. Then I, her vassal, am subject to her mood and whim.

Not possible, you say? A mother would never be like that to her daughter? I laugh. She is a witch – a goylem disguised as a mother – which makes me, her issue, a blacker more hideous version of the same.

I will say it here where for all time it will be known that never while I breathe a breath shall I bring forth into life another human being, especially not a girl.

Why has God made woman? To serve *man* – who does as he will – who is created in God's image. She is put on earth to be his servant and his whore. Thank you, God – that makes me a perfect woman.

And why then have you made my mother? To make sure that my life continues to be as atrocious as it can possibly be? ...God?

19 Tamuz, 5549
July 13, 1789

Something immense happened today!

I'm excited and nervous. I talked with Reb Thanhausser! Imagine, seven years without a word and today we looked at each other and spoke to each other. I'm glad I have this book to write in.

about it. Here's what happened:

I knew that the bookseller would have his cart in town this very day. How did I know? He told me last month that it takes him three weeks exactly to make the rounds of villages. The weather hasn't been a problem – we haven't had big storms. So from the marks I've kept in my book of days I knew today was the day.

I tried to get to market early to keep from seeing many others as I always do. Before the night had fully faded I gathered my basket, pulled my shawl over my head and set out. My mother either sleeps her days away or sits at the table and drinks beer and since it was early when I left she was still asleep.

I bought a loaf of bread, a beef bone and some vegetables for stew. There wasn't much to choose from but I can make due with whatever's around. I'm a pretty fair cook. At the inn we serve good food but nothing fancy.

I walked to the other end of the street to find the bookseller but he was not in his usual place. I was wondering where he was and just as I turned to head home I collided with a man. I must have been looking down. I never saw him until we bumped and even then I didn't want to look him in the face. I stay as far away from men as possible.

The man apologized over and over. When I heard his voice I recognized him – Reb Thanhausser! I dared to look at him and oh happiness, it was Samuel's teacher. It wasn't the first time I've seen him but in all these years I've only spotted him from a distance. I have always avoided him.

So a fast shiver zigzagged through me, my eyes teared up and directly I was standing on the edge of a knife. I knew if I said one word I would burst into tears. I really have not felt such a strong thing... not for a long time.

I turned to walk away – my true cowardice on perfect display. But he stepped around and stood in front of me. We stared at each other for ten minutes – or what felt like it – before he finally said something. All I could think was: seven years have passed and I still feel like a nine year old.

He looked at me so hard that his eyes turned red and filled with tears – and they vibrated! When I saw that, things roped up into knots inside. He talked softly but I heard him:

'Marta... Marta... it's you! Shalom, my dear.' He choked up when he said my name and he peered right into me.

Inside of me: big flip-flops. I was sick to my stomach. Little sparks of light flew around my eyes and I got dizzy. Was I going to retch right there in the market?

'Marta?'

He broke into my thoughts and I was happy to look up and see him still standing there. I smiled at him, he smiled back. Then we grinned at each other for another ten minutes... maybe an exaggeration.

I remembered how nice Reb Thanhausser had been to me. He was one of the few people other than Samuel who ever took time to talk with me. So when he said my name and looked at me like that I couldn't help myself... I sobbed like a baby right there at the market in front of everyone.

While I fumbled around in my pocket for a cloth Reb Thanhausser escorted me out of the market up behind the tailor's to the path that runs along the creek behind the houses. I tried to stop crying but I couldn't. I was so verklempt from the whole thing that I sat down on the riverbank and bawled until I felt empty.

When I finally looked up he was still there sitting beside me, half-smiling. Here's what he said:

'Marta Lindauer. I seem to find myself shoring

you up from under your tears once again. Hmm? Do you remember the last time we talked when you were nine? You had a sad story, indeed. Now you must be what, sixteen?'

The tenderness in his voice melted me again. Tears came up from my deepest heart – I could not stop crying. I saw a clear memory of Samuel running around like a goof in the garden. He was so cute and funny and he had such beautiful curly hair. My big brother – and now I'm older than he ever was. Life has a strange way.

I cried so much I felt sick so finally I had to pull myself together. I was a blubbering mess. I'm sure my nose was big and red and my eyes were swollen and ugly. I needed to get home and get to work but everything inside me said... stay.

I apologized for my embarrassing behavior. Reb Thanhausser told me in the same calm voice I remembered that I had nothing to apologize *for*. Here's what he said next:

'Marta, I'm not surprised that you can't stop crying. You must have seven years' worth of tears stored up inside of you...'

Of course he was right. I do have sadness in me but I swallow it down over and over. I never cry. So I just nodded to let him know I heard him. Then

I stood up to walk back to the inn and he stood, too.

'Let me walk you home, Marta,' he said. 'It is good to see you again. You have grown up and become a lovely young woman.'

His voice and manners were soft and his eyes held their usual kindness. But little did he know: although I may look lovely, which isn't true either, deep down inside I am a lying and devious person who deserves all bad things. Couldn't he see the ugliness in me?

Then I brushed off my skirt and adjusted my kerchief. I didn't know what else to say. I wouldn't have minded talking with him – I think I might have liked it – but I didn't want to be seen with him or anyone in public. I don't want any more rumors spread about me in Jebenhausen. I told him this:

'Reb Thanhausser, you can see that you've had a strong effect on me. Now I need to collect myself and get on with my day. Thank you for being with me just now. I really am sorry for being such a crybaby...' and on and on with more of the same.

I tried not to look at him because I was saying stupid things and also because his face wore such a tender expression that I wasn't sure I could hold myself together – he was too kind. It made me feel ridiculous. Someone as hideous as I am does not deserve that.

Before I fell apart again I rushed away from him. I don't think I even said goodbye. But he called to me.

'Marta, may I see you again?'

I stopped and turned and a long stream of warnings ran through my mind. But a voice inside me that usually remains silent said yes. I nodded once. He smiled and raised his hand and then I turned toward home.

Today was a beautiful morning, mild and breezy, bluest sky, new bright green leaves on the trees, so many lovely flowers and bushes in bloom.

As I walked down the hill I looked up and saw a huge and magnificent bird – maybe it was an eagle – soaring above me. It circled around and flew out over the valley then gave a sharp call and suddenly there was another one – it's mate! I watched them weave through the air together until they were specks in the distance.

Seeing that bird reminded me of once when an eagle looked right at me when I was little – sitting by the pond. And then I remembered that Reb Thanhausser was sitting beside me when it happened.

My memory from then connected with my life today. It felt like a message from God... that maybe it's all right that I'm still alive. Maybe there *is* a reason for me to live. Maybe I'm not completely repugnant. Sometimes I dare to imagine there might be a tiny piece of me that's good.

So much happened even before breakfast. I haven't had one calm thought all day. Tomorrow I'm going to the market again early. I want to see if the bookseller will be there and maybe I'll see Reb Thanhausser again, too. It's true he's a man but he seems different from the rest.

26 Tamuz, 5549
July 20, 1789

Some days I'm too tired at the end of the day to write. And some mornings I sleep too late and must get right to my work. It's been raining for nearly a week and everything is muddy and soggy.

Yes the fields and trees and grasses and flowers love it and so do the biting insects. Now the whole world smells of mildew. I've been to the market every morning but I haven't seen either the bookseller or Reb Thanhausser. Where are they?

Yesterday I made a visit to Babette at the

mikveh, the ritual bath. According to Jewish law I'm not required to go there until I'm married. Since I plan never to be any man's wife I'll never need to use it. But I do sometimes require a visit with Babette because she's the only person in town other than Reb Veberke who'll talk with me.

Her nose is in everyone's business and for the women who go to the mikveh she makes a necessary ritual seem better than it actually is. I would hate taking off my clothes and dipping down in that well. It's FREEZING water. All last winter women took sick afterwards. I know they're supposed to feel cleansed and sanctified from it but all I would ever feel if I had to dunk under that icy water is wretched – I hate being cold.

There's talk about building a better house for it with a stove so that at least the women aren't perishing from exposure. The small structure we have now is built directly over the stream so the women step onto the ledge into ice-cold water and then get out into the ice-cold air. Sonia Einstein passed away last winter after taking ill from this very thing – and she was only twenty. God made woman too, but it's not so easy.

Babette is from the Weil family. She married a nephew of Moishe Weil the Learned. When I visit her at the mikveh she cleans my fingernails and brushes my hair like a sister might although she's nicer than my real sister.

Babette's also a *shadchan*... she helps arrange marriages. Yesterday she hinted to me that there's a man who's interested in me!

Well when she said it my insides turned and heaved and I felt like I might throw up. She said she would talk with my mother about it.

The only problem is that my mother is not easy to talk with. When she's awake she's screeching at me. And the rest of the time she's sleeping off her latest bout of drinking. She's been like this for years ever since Samuel died.

If I just assume that she's not available to help do anything that makes my job running the inn easier. If I don't expect anything from her then I'm not disappointed that she doesn't do anything.

Back to this man that Babette mentioned... I asked her who he is but she wouldn't tell me. She said she should talk with my mother first.

A panic grew inside me when she said that because I never want to be married – ever! I don't want to be a wife. I don't want to be some man's wife so he can... well I just don't ever want to do it. I know that according to God's law I'm supposed to want to get married and have children. But I don't want to.

I try to be invisible. I stay out of sight of the townspeople as much as possible. I wish they would forget about me. Why can't people leave me alone?

Still, I had to know more from her. Here's how our talk went:

Me: Is there any way for me not to marry this man?

Babette: Why? You don't even know who he is. He's a good prospect, Marta. He's not too old and he has some money. You'll be better off than you are now. You could have a better life than you have now, working so hard at the inn.

Me: (Here's where my voice got shaky.) There's no money for a dowry for me. I don't mind my life the way it is. I don't ... (I didn't know what to say.) ... I don't care to be married.

Babette looked surprised... I surprised myself. That was the first time I had ever said those words to anyone even though I've known it was true since Samuel died.

Babette: I'm surprised, Marta. I would have thought that you would jump at the chance to leave that inn and your life there behind.

Me: I would rather do honest hard work to sustain my mother and myself than be any man's wife. I mean It, Babette.

Babette: Well dear one (she laughed here) you'll still be doing plenty of honest hard work when you're married. But your status will rise. You'll no longer be a pariah. Tell me, are you happy now with things the way they are?

Everyone in town knows what happened to me. Well they don't know all the details but they know enough... enough to treat me like I have a catching disease.

Me: I don't care about being happy. I'm fine. I just know that I don't ever want to be married... I don't like men.

Babette: Don't be ridiculous – you need to let the past be in the past. This man I'm talking about is a good man. He's a mensch and he's seen you and he wants to meet you.

Me: No! (I stamped my foot.) My answer is no.

I gathered my shawl and tried to leave but Babette blocked my way.

Babette: Marta, you should meet this man. You might find that he's not so bad. (I just shook my head – no!) Never mind your willfulness... I'm going to call on your mother soon. When would be a good time?

What could I possibly say to that? Everyone knows I run the inn, not my mother. The only time she has any control over herself is in the morning before she starts drinking. But she's always always in a bad mood.

Me: You can try her early in the day. But, I'm telling you... I won't be that man's wife... I won't!

Babette: Well, let me talk to her and we'll see how it goes. I think you don't know yourself very well, Marta. A good man can make a woman very happy... it's a fulfillment of God's commandment...

... And on and on. She said he's a horse dealer from Ulm who comes to town to trade but she wouldn't tell me any more about him.

Oh my head aches just thinking about it. The thing is, she says I don't know myself and that may be true. But she doesn't know me either. There's darkness in me – down in my depths. I have evil thoughts. I fight against living. Besides, why would any man want me? I'm ugly and dirty and ruined. Once he learns who I really am he'll run away... fast... I hope.

28 Tamuz, 5549
July 22, 1789

I love writing in my book. I like to go back and read what I've already written. Even though I write small I'll need a much bigger book if I'm to tell all.

There is more going on in my life these days than went on altogether for the past seven years. Nothing happened for so long now everything's happening. I found this paper and pen and made my book just in time to write about it. I haven't had so many stomach aches for a long time.

I went to the market early this morning like I always do. I had just finished buying vegetables when I noticed that the bookseller was back. While he talked with Jakob ben Likht, the candle maker, I stood nearby and waited for them to finish.

I overheard some other men talking about France. They said the peasants are going to rise up against the King and Queen. I suppose it would take many peasants to overpower the armies of the rulers. I never want to be in a war. What a horrible thing – everyone running through the land hating and killing each other. Life is hard enough – why make it worse?

The bookseller told me that he was held up in Sussen because his mother took ill but she recovered. I traded one of my books for another from him, more morality stories. They help me understand about how to live, how to live as a good God-fearing woman when deep down I know I'm not.

What other people see when they look at me is a different person from the one who lives inside my skin. Also those stories take me to new places in my imagination away from my regular life.

Reb Thanhausser walked up to the bookseller's cart just as I was leaving. We nodded a greeting – inside me... a shiver. I pretended to pick through some greens that were piled on a table nearby while he did his business and then when he began to walk away I stepped over into his path. I know it wasn't proper but I didn't care – I wanted to see him again.

When I heard his calm voice, something ragged in me was smoothed. He smiled at me and here's what he said:

'Good morning, Marta. How nice to see you again.'

He made a little bow and I did a curtsey back to him. I felt my face heat up and suddenly I was all jittery inside... everything in me was trembling. I was so affected by his greeting.... Why? After all, all he did was say hello. I couldn't even talk! Luckily, he kept the conversation going.

'May I have the honor of escorting you for a walk?' Here he looked around at all the people who were milling about the market making purchases and talking to each other. He lifted his eyebrows at me with a twinkle in his eye.

'I'm sure there is much for us to share – that is, if you are interested in conversing with me...?'

So many warning voices and a loud buzz in my head... it was hard to think with all that going on. But I didn't listen to those voices and I didn't care. Just then I wanted to talk with him.

I nodded to let him know I would do it – that is, go for a walk with him. He asked me if 'now would be a good time' and I nodded yes again. I'll tell you... my stomach seized up and I thought for sure that I would need to rush off... but I managed all right.

He took me by the elbow and escorted me – in front of everyone – up the Boller Strasse toward the inn but before we got there he turned off between two houses and we ended up on the mountain path. I tucked my basket into some weeds beside a post so I could get it on the way back.

I hadn't been up there for years. My work at the inn left me no time for indulgent walks. It was beautiful though. I loved the way the wind blew the grasses around into ripples and waves - like music flowing – like grand flocks of birds aloft.

Everything was alive and moving. Little bugs flew around and caught the light as though they were lit up. And a fox and its most adorable babies played on a mound of dirt in the sunshine. We saw hawks and that same pair of eagles from before, I'm sure. What a splendid view of the valley from the side of the mountain… I'd forgotten. I had to wipe away a few tears.

I was so enthralled with the beauty of everything that I forgot to be nervous around Reb Thanhausser. He pointed out the place in the hedge where I used to go through with Samuel when we were little. I went there before with him, too. I hadn't thought about Heaven for so many years. Samuel and I called it that. We used to sneak away to Heaven and play fairies. We pretended that the fairies were our friends and that we were fairies, too.

Reb Thanhausser asked me if I wanted to go in but I surely did not so we climbed higher until we were at the pond – the same pond where I saw that eagle up close a long time ago. I used to go there when I needed to be alone back when I was little.

The path to the pond was overgrown but we managed to stomp some grass down so we could sit close to the water. We sat for a while before either one of us said anything. I had no idea where to begin so I waited for him to start. I can't remember exactly what we both said but this is pretty close:

Reb Thanhausser: Where do we even start, eh?

He sat away from me, far enough that I didn't feel uncomfortable being there with him. I found I liked being there with him. He looks older – it's been seven years since I've seen him up close but he looked nice to me... soft brown eyes and wavy brown hair, a long beard and moustache.

Reb Thanhausser has what I would call a strong nose but not a huge one. He has thin lips but you can't see them very well because of his moustache. One thing I remember from before and it's still true is that he has rosy cheeks. He's thin and taller than I am but he's not a very tall man.

I like the way he looks. He has a twinkle in his eye and a pleasant manner. And his teeth still look alright. I had no idea where to begin so I asked him a question.

Me: Are you still teaching at the school?

Reb T: Yes, it's going well. We have twenty-seven students and nine of them are girls, Marta. Why don't you come? I think you would enjoy learning German and arithmetic, don't you agree?

Me: I don't need to learn arithmetic. I can add and subtract and do receipts... what else do I need numbers for? And my German's pretty good already.

I was cautious answering his question because I don't want to go to school. Most girls my age are either married or about to be. I'd feel foolish being so much older than the others.

Me: Besides, I don't have time – I have too much to do. As it is I'm going to be behind on everything at home.

I wondered why I felt embarrassed. Was it because of the way he was looking at me?

Reb T: All right, I won't pressure you.

He looked around and neither of us said anything for a few minutes. I relaxed and felt trust, like a bridge, take form between us. It was a feeling I remembered from when he lived in the inn when I was small. I had that same flicker of light kept alive deep within my soul by being near him.

Reb T: Marta, tell me about yourself. I understand that you have responsibility for the running of the inn. Is that correct?

Me: Yes.

I had little to say.

Reb T: And, your mother? How does she fare?

Me: Oh, well... she's the same.

Reb T: The same as before, when I was there?

I wasn't sure I wanted to tell him the truth even though everyone in town probably knows about my mother. I decided that since I almost never talk with anyone else except Babette a little, I would trust him and go ahead and tell him some things.

Me: She drinks... to excess... every day. And yes she's as crabby as ever whether she's drunk or not.

Reb T: I'm sorry to hear that. So, it must not be easy for you, living and working with her.

Me: She doesn't work.

He raised his eyebrows in surprise.

Reb T: Not at all?

Me: Not really, no. I do everything.

There was a great deal of staring directed at me... to the point that I became uncomfortable.

Me: Reb Thanhausser, why do you keep looking at me like that? Is there something wrong with my face?

He smiled! And that made me certain that there was a problem with my face. I was ashamed and mixed-up so I stood and turned away from him to leave. Then he jumped up and came around in front of me and faced me. I didn't want him to look at me so I ducked and headed out toward the big path. And of course he followed.

Reb T: Marta... wait! There is nothing wrong with your face! I promise... please wait.

I felt like a stupid child and tried to hurry away from him but he caught up with me. For the second time he ran around in front of me and stood in my way. I wanted to disappear. I knew I was ugly.

Reb T: Marta, your face is beautiful. You're beautiful. I'm taken with what a handsome young woman you have become, that is all. Please stay and talk with me. I promise I won't stare at you.

I know that Reb Thanhausser meant well but just then I was upset and needed to get back to the inn where I knew I could pull myself together. I started walking but he kept up. I tried to shoo him away.

Me: It's alright. I need to get home. I have lots of work to do today.

Reb T: Do you mind if I walk with you? I enjoy your company and I would like to hear more about you.

I wanted him to go away. I'm certain he was mocking me when he said those things. Beautiful? Handsome? Ridiculous is more like it. I walked as fast as I could but I felt myself going down inside, down into my dark cave of existence. I don't remember what he said to me after that because all I heard in my own head was what a stupid ugly girl I am. And how foolish I was to think I could actually carry on a conversation with a man.

I spent the day working as hard as I could trying to get away from pounding thoughts that would *not* go away. After I fed the guests, cleaned up and put my mother to bed, I came upstairs and wrote these pages.

There is something very ugly inside of me – like the ugliest witch or the creepiest spider or the worst thing you can imagine.

No one else sees this ugliness inside of me I hope. People mostly see the faces I wear to try to keep it from showing.

29 Tamuz, 5549
July 23, 1789

Now everything is dark. I can't see anything good. I'm full of hate. I hate myself, I hate my mother, I hate being alive. I always end up like this.

I went to the market to buy a few onions and some lentils. I wish people would leave me alone. I heard that rude man whisper something under his breath so I leaned toward him and asked him what he had said. When he talked at me his foul breath nearly knocked me over.

He said, 'Anything else, zoyne?'

I set the onions back down on the table and the bag of lentils, too. I felt my face get hot then I turned around and rushed home.

Of course when I got here my mother was furious that I didn't have the lentils and onions so she called me zoyne too and since there's nothing else she can take away from me or punish me with she proceeded to rant and yell for fifteen minutes like she always does.

I used to cry when she did that because she scared me. But now I'm taller than she is and she knows I'm strong. If she tries to hit me like she used to, I grab her wrists to keep her from hurting me.

Once I took hold of her wrists and wrestled her arms down until she had to kneel on the floor. When she stood up she was so angry that she slapped my face hard and kicked my shin. I was tempted to slap her back but I didn't do it. Inside I boiled.

When I get like this the whole world goes black. I don't understand why I am even alive. Maybe just to do a lot of work.

6 Av, 5549
July 29, 1789

Babette Weil came by early this morning. They talked, she and my mother, and now this man named David Ferd Soykher will call on me on Sunday. Never before have I stepped out with a man for the purpose of considering marriage. I'm filled with dread.

Twice there were men who approached my mother but she wasn't ready to let me go and I can't figure out why she is now – not that I want to get married.

I'll meet him but that is all. I won't pretend anything. He's going to get my true honest responses... God help me.

14 Av, 5549
Aug 6, 1789

MY EARLIER DAYS

It was my Bubby who died next but first I want to write about my brother, Samuel. Samuel and I felt like we had always been brother and sister – all through time – and always would be even after we died.

When he left me and his earthly life behind I thought a lot about dying. Dying is not so bad. We go back to God which can only be good. The bad part is we leave behind people who love us and who will miss us while they finish out their lives here in life. When I die no one will be sorry to see me go.

But Samuel was funny. He made stupid jokes that forced me to smile and he was always so nice to me. I miss him every day.

16 Av, 5549
Aug 8, 1789

How powerful words are. I remembered his jokes and then I couldn't help myself – I cried for a long time and couldn't write any more. This from a girl who does not cry. Today I want to write about when Samuel died. I haven't talked about this with anyone ever.

Like I said he taught me to read and write and understand numbers and always made me feel better. He was only twelve, almost thirteen, when he died and I was nine.

For a long time after I couldn't believe that it had really happened. I kept imagining he would come back. Sometimes I missed him so much my head hurt and my chest ached and I would curl up on my bed and rock back and forth.

I missed my violin too. I used to play the violin. I missed it so much. I lost them both at the same time... my brother and my music.

After that it felt like the bottom had fallen out and I was left dangling from a thread over a black void... and that's how I was supposed to live. I guess it's how I have lived. I've gotten good at swinging blindly over nothingness.

Being a Jew doesn't seem to fix it either. In my meanest and worst moods nothing helps. If God is so merciful why did Samuel have to die and why is my violin gone? Why do I have my mother and why do I feel bad so much of the time?

I don't remember much about the days after

Samuel died except that I wanted to shrivel up and die, myself. I wanted the wind to blow me away. My mind actually did float away – I went crazy for a while. Even when I finally got up to work again my mind was far far away. I was a ghost floating through my own life.

The night he died he had a fever and was thrashing in his bed. I tried to keep a cool compress on him but he kept knocking my hand away. He didn't know what he was doing, from the fever. We changed the sheets so many times I lost count. Mother, Hindel and I did everything we could think of... the barber-surgeon, too.

Samuel finally calmed down – he was in a trance. He was seeing something but it was only in his imagination. It was late in the night, maybe early morning – it was still dark out. Even in the candlelight I could tell how pale he was. He had given up – there wasn't much left of him.

I had hold of one hand and my mother had the other. She rubbed his arm, squeezed his hand and then she climbed onto the bed next to him and hugged her whole body up next to his. She pleaded with him: 'Samuel, Samuel my darling boy... wake up... don't leave me!' She prayed to the Lord. She was crying. I am too right now.

Just before the worst happened he turned his face toward me. I remember tears in his eyes. His lips were dry and cracked and peeling and his face was the color of bad bread – gray and green. He scarcely had energy to talk so I leaned my ear up to his mouth. Then in the softest whisper he said: 'Heaven...'

I looked hard into his eyes. I felt myself get strong for him. He was trying to tell me something and I wanted to help him. I said:

'Yes you will be in heaven soon, Samuel. And I promise I'll meet you there when it's my turn to die. You'll see father and grandmother and everybody.' I was crying.

Samuel grimaced and tried to say something else but he couldn't. I saw his body shudder, then he struggled, then he choked, then he took a deep breath – his last – and then he exhaled his life away. I saw his spirit leave him.

I don't remember what happened next. I went into a long swoon, a descent into a sad sad bleak place. I've never talked with anyone about this. I'm glad to have these pages to write in.

We lost Samuel that night and my violin disappeared too. It just disappeared. And so my music days were over.

When I think about it all too much despair settles over me like a heavy quilt and weighs me down. I have trouble getting out of bed. Some days everything looks so black to me when I wake up that the whole day ends up feeling wrong and crooked all day long.

It wasn't as awful as I expected – writing about Samuel. Thinking about him isn't as hard as it used to be. I should have been the one who died though.

I'd better go. If I don't get the cholent started we'll have nothing to serve for Shabbos.

And I have to see that man day after tomorrow. I shall wash my face for him but that's all.

17 Av, 5549
August 9, 1789
early morning

Huge storm last night or early this morning with three bright flashes and immediate sharp thunderclaps that woke me. I hid under the covers for a long time even though it was hot in there. I hate storms. It's still early now, I haven't even gone to the market yet. I write by candlelight waiting for daylight.

Mixed in with my usual planning for the day I've been thinking about David Ferd Soykher. When I try to imagine being a man's wife I can't do it. I could do all the necessary household work... God knows I'm good at it. But the part of my imaginings where he... fulfills his marriage covenant – and I would have to too – is something I can't picture. I cannot see myself going along with that. When I try to imagine being with a man that way there are too many ghastly images that rush in to blot it out.

Dear Fraynd, you do not know anything of my past. You listen to everything I have to say and make no comment or complaint. I wish I could erase all of those memories. They rise up from a locked and hidden closet deep within me – they won't leave me alone... ever. And they remind me of what a dishonorable person I am and how I shall never be happy because I am no good. I am ugly and evil and everyone knows it.

17 Av, 5549
August 9, 1789
late night

Well, this day turned out much different than I expected. After I wrote this morning I set out for the market. There was a hovering fog that made everything damp and cool so I wrapped a shawl over my head and made my way down the hill. Just as I arrived at the market Reb Thanhausser stepped up beside me.

I didn't let on but I was pleased to see him – a peculiar feeling in me. He leaned toward me and walked with his hands folded behind his back just like he always does. And seeing his gestures and the way he carries himself, well... I don't have the same need to guard myself around him the way I do around other men. It's because I remember him so well from when I was little. He was always so nice to me... he still is.

After we greeted he asked me if I would be able to walk with him again – hopefully up the mountain path like we did before. I knew that if I answered yes, which I did want to do, I would be handling his request badly.

Everyone knows that if he wants to talk with me further, no matter how innocent his request, he must clear it with my mother first. I said something to that effect but his reply was firm: He did not want to have any words with my mother... not ever if humanly possible. I stopped short when he said that. He looked right at me:

'Marta, you have already walked with me twice

before. Can we not continue to meet and converse without the approval of your mother? My intentions are completely honorable, you know. I so enjoy your company just as I did when you were a girl. I would like to hear more about you and what you are thinking about…' He went on like this until I interrupted.

'Reb Thanhausser, please don't think that I don't want to walk with you… I do, very much. But it isn't right. If we're noticed I'll surely be chastised. And my reputation will suffer further; I'll be even more despicable in the eyes of others than I already am.'

He stopped walking, clasped his hands together and leaned his head back to look up toward the heavens. Then he looked right at me and his eyes were vibrating again, the same as before!

'Marta, Marta,' he said. I felt caught as a bug in a web. 'My need to converse with you is stronger than any social directive.'

At that, he took my elbow and turned me away from the market along a path between two buildings and back to our original meeting place beside the creek. I had no argument against his sentiment so I submitted and went along.

We stood for a moment beside the stream and

watched a goose waddle up to the edge for a drink. I waited for Reb Thanhausser to speak.

'You are not despicable, Marta. You are a lovely and talented young woman. Although wicked things happened to you when you were younger, they are now long over with. You deserve to have a life with some degree of happiness in it.'

He said more things like that but they all sounded like platitudes and meaningless jabber. Although I had never heard those words spoken before they bounced right off me and landed in the mud.

Whatever he thinks I deserve, he's wrong. I deserve nothing. My behavior as a child was shameful and inexcusable and all I really deserve is a small life filled with hard work so I might redeem myself in God's eyes. That's all I care about – what God will do with me when I die. My life here in Jebenhausen is temporary and hopefully short-lived. I long to be away from it. What I said was:

'Reb Thanhausser, as you might remember I'm not a very good follower of rules either. Even though my life is already so broken that it probably doesn't matter what I do, I've spent the last seven years trying to avoid notice wherever I go. That's why I think we shouldn't walk together. It's not because I don't want to... please understand that... I do enjoy visiting with you.'

It was easy saying those things to him. He smiled then and I did, too.

'Marta, come spend some time with me. Consider this: since people think badly of you already, what does it matter what they'll think if we walk up the mountain together?'

We watched a spotted dog run out from behind a house to chase after the goose which had been minding its own business in the grass. The huge bird stopped and turned on the dog, spread its formidable wings and honked and squawked until the dog ran off.

Was that a lesson for me?

I needed to shop and get home to get breakfast on for my mother and our guests. But that normally silent little voice inside me piped up again. She said: 'If you agree with him then go ahead and see him. He's right... what could it hurt?' The conflict inside of me didn't take long to resolve...

'Alright Reb Thanhausser. I'll meet with you. But it will have to be later this afternoon before I make dinner.'

I admit to a thrill. It had been a long time since

I'd engaged in a deception... seven years in fact!

The man was happy. When he smiled his face was filled with light. I hadn't seen that kind of thing for so long – I had to turn away so he wouldn't see my emotions. I don't know why I did that... tear up I mean. Maybe it's because I'm not used to happiness.

We made our plans and then I shopped and continued with my day. The hours refused to pass at normal speed – they went much too slow. When I slipped out through the garden this afternoon I found him waiting by the gate to the back path.

Before I write about our walk I should mention that Babette stopped by after the noonday meal so she could see if all was ready for the meeting with David Ferd Soykher tomorrow.

I'm good at having people think I'm interested in something even when I'm not so it wasn't hard to convince her that all is in order for the man's visit. It was another deception for me to do that so I'm doubly cursed for the day – but I don't care. I don't care about Ferd Soykher and I don't care what people will think of me – no matter what I do. Nothing really matters anyway.

My mother was in rare form for Babette's visit. Have you ever seen how a wretched drunk behaves by early afternoon? She calls me zoyne now as her own personal endearment – she has no interest in my feelings or desires but when I am honest – she never did.

All the words she directs toward me are venomous and acidic which provokes a mean response from me. I hope I'm not as awful and nasty a person as she is but when I'm around her I turn into someone just like her.

Apparently there is some money for a dowry for me even though I never knew about it. And it appears I have little say in whether or not I will accept or decline this man's proposal. Both women seem to think he will be the answer to their prayers. Too bad he's not the answer to mine. I can't stand my mother. She makes me sick...

I couldn't wait for Babette to leave so I could see Reb Thanhausser. That's not how I usually feel about her but today was unusual in so many ways.

We walked quickly to get out of view of anyone else and then slowed down. I put tomorrow's meeting out of my mind – sealed it up in a locked cupboard for a little while.

I loved walking on that path, climbing higher and seeing farther and farther out over the land. Everything was so pleasant – the breeze, the birds, the grasses blowing in the fields, the orchards in rows... everything. Even the temperature was delightful.

I needed only my dress, no sweater or shawl. I went bareheaded and let my braid fall loose. I ran and skipped and turned in circles. I even laughed! Reb Thanhausser was watching me but I didn't care at all. What freedom! How long since I'd felt that way?

When we got to the spot on the path that led to Heaven he asked me if I wanted to go in. I must have been feeling brave because I said: 'Alright why not?' And after we trampled down some viney undergrowth and tore away some branches we went into the place I haven't seen since Samuel died.

Oh how can I describe it? So quiet, so peaceful, so beautiful... a thick springy rug of pine needles, tall majestic trees, massive beeches, sunlight dancing through high branches. Sounds in there were muffled and amplified at the same time.

I walked in ahead of Reb Thanhausser with Samuel's memory keeping step beside me. We had such good times together there hiding from everyone else in the world in our fairyland.

At first I felt sad and I did cry a little. But after that I was all right. I was glad to be there again with Reb Thanhausser.

He walked over to the biggest tree, the one with the huge hole at the bottom and right next to it was the same little hillock that we used to sit on. Nothing had changed... only me.

I felt older than ever and younger than I had in a long long time... both feelings at once. I told you this was an unusual day.

He sat on the bump while I walked around under the trees remembering Samuel and marveling at the loveliness and serenity. When I was ready, I sat down at the foot of the big tree like I used to do. Reb Thanhausser's gaze stayed on my face which made me uncomfortable – no one else looks at me like that. Then we talked. Here's how it went – or close to it:

He started. 'Marta, here we are again.' His eyes looked sad but they still had that twinkle.

Even though my head swirled with thoughts it wasn't easy to know what to say. Seven years have passed yet I felt just as mixed up and stupid as I did when I was nine.

He tried again.

'Please, tell me something about yourself, Marta. What are your interests? I understand that you read. But, what else do you do to occupy your active mind?'

I just laughed.

'Ha! Are you joking? I work sir... sun up to sun down, every day of the year. I work at the inn...' For proof I held out my hands for him to see – chapped, calloused, full of burns and cuts and scars.

In the colder weather I get cracks in the skin at the corners of my fingernails that split open and are so painful whenever I use my hands which is always.

He reached out and took hold of them and that shocked me. I pulled away but he held on. I felt his warmth. Then he looked into my eyes or into my soul I should say. I didn't know what to do. He stared at me for a long time. I was caught in the power of his eyes – vibrating and watering, deep dark sad – saying so much to me.

He began to speak but burst into sobs instead. He still held my hands – I couldn't let go – and he sat in front of me looking at me the whole time, weeping. But it was not just crying – it was more like a plea. A swell of tenderness toward him grew in me.

I dug a cloth out of my pocket so he could wipe his nose and waited for him to say something which he finally did.

'Your hands, Marta. I remember what these hands accomplished when you were small.'

Well I did too but I had never said or heard a word from anyone about the subject until that moment except what I've written here in my book.

A great turbulence lurched through me. I thought I would be sick. He grabbed my hands again and held on and I was forced to stay seated. I squinted and sneered at him – like a cornered animal – but he was resolute. His eyes were full of tears and I was flooded with anger. I was seething... I didn't like being restrained.

Then he talked to me and hearing his voice calmed me down. I can't remember what he was saying because there was a clamor in my head but I was finally able to sit quietly and would you believe it he brought it up again!

'You played that violin like an angel, Marta. You showed me that you have very special gifts, indeed.' He emphasized his words by shaking my hands up and down. 'Those gifts are from God and they live in a person their whole life. It's part of who they are. They're born with them.' Then, he looked right at me expecting me to say something.

Now... my violin and that time in my life is gone. I don't want to think about it – not yet. I'm not ready. I sputtered some answer like: 'It's all gone... it doesn't matter anymore,' things like that. I managed to pull my hands back and tried to look anywhere but at him.

The grove where we sat was silent and so were we for several long moments... maybe minutes. I was thinking about writing in my book about Heaven and also about how much I love to write and how much it means to me to have paper and quill.

Right now my candle is nearly burned down – it's late in the night – probably morning already and later on today I'm to meet Ferd Soykher... oy vey.

I wondered if I should tell him about my book as a way to change the subject. So I did.

'Reb Thanhausser, I've been doing some writing.'

He nodded and grabbed my eyes again.

'Good, Marta. That is good news. Tell me, what is your subject matter?'

I told him about finding the paper and ink pen and making my book, about my visit to Reb Veberke (to this he said 'That man is a treasure') and how I spend hours every night and many mornings recording my thoughts. I was surprised at what he said next.

'Would you ever let me read what you have written?'

I'm sure I looked horrified. These words are for me alone. Putting them down on paper has made me feel like I'm somewhat alive again, like I matter – to myself, at least. And the freedom I feel when I write what I must only exists because of my assurance to myself that no one else will ever read my words... ever.

"I should say not sir... Never...." I watched him closely to see what his reaction would be.

Reb Thanhausser slowly nodded and then grinned back at me – even his eyes were smiling – and I remembered how he always used to behave in the exact opposite manner from my mother and sister. He and Samuel were like that. His smile loosened the tightness inside me so I smiled, too.

And then, gazing into his eyes, I realized something... that he and I have a secret pact! I believed just then that I could say anything to him and it would be alright.

I don't fool myself into believing this is actually

true but it's how I felt then. I wasn't thinking of him as a regular man. He felt like the kind of dream friend that you are, Fraynd... the kind who sees you overall as a good person which is something that you yourself can't see.

His soul and my soul understood each other and my crazy mind was buzzing like cicadas but that wasn't what was really happening. What was happening was that he and I were sharing something true between us and something bigger than both of us. It felt like a message from God passing between us, pure and good.

He took my hands again and then the most awkward thing happened. When I looked at him and saw his kind face I started to tremble and I couldn't stop. In seconds I was shaking so much that I had to draw my hands back and stand up. Of course Reb T also stood – right in front of me. I was embarrassed to have him see my face and I wanted to turn away but I also didn't want to.

'Marta, dearest Marta... I felt it, too!'

I was holding myself together with my arms wishing I could stop shaking all over. I wasn't cold. In fact it was warm out.

He took hold of my shoulders, pulled me close and then wrapped his arms around me. The top of my head came just to his chin so I laid my cheek against his chest. I even put my arms around him. I could hear his heart beating. For a few moments none of this felt wrong. Once I calmed down and stopped trembling he stepped back away from me.

I'm going to try to describe what he looked like to me just then: he was the most beautiful creature who ever walked on earth. His entire countenance was lit up. His eyes, oh those eyes! They were saying a great deal to me. Then in some small distant and guarded part of me something let go... and I understood the compassion his beautiful eyes were sharing with me.

But the me who was standing there in Heaven remembered that it was getting late and I needed to get home to fix dinner. So in the hubbub of my thoughts I sought escape, although it wasn't easy to talk. What do you say after something like that? I was still reeling and I assumed he was, too. I decided to say nothing. What happened between us was the kind of thing that words are useless for.

We stood there in the quiet of the grove and once we had both gathered ourselves he offered me his arm and we walked out together, at least until we got to the brambly part.

Outside of Heaven life was still going on around

us as usual – soft wind and clouds and farmers on the distant hills, travelers on the road, the town below us. Once on the way down he stopped, took my hand, pulled it to his breast and leaned his head back. It looked like he was praying and I don't doubt it. Reb Thanhausser is a man of God, this I know. Anyone who's that kind and good - he's a man of God.

I'm too tired to write any more tonight. I will always remember this day. Come along my comrade sleep... let's join together and pretend that daylight will not come.

18 Av, 5549
August 10, 1789

Daylight came after all along with the certainty of my impending doom. Hair, teeth, face... plain dress. Ran to market – cool misty morning. Saw no one thank goodness.

Babette was here when I returned and they were carrying on as though the deal was done and toasted to. Babette had lots of smiles although I couldn't come up with one for her.

He would arrive early, there would be introductions, I would accompany him on a walk.

My stomach was hardened into a tight bunch which made it hard to breathe. And my head hurt.

I carried on with my tasks until I heard a horse clomp up to the inn. I was upstairs but stayed near the front window. Here's what I saw when I looked down: A beautiful huge draft horse, a bay, with a man climbing down. The man looked small next to the horse but I couldn't see his face.

The horse had a thick high arched neck, a crooked blaze and white feathered fetlocks that covered its hooves. Its rump was big and round and it had a short mane and a short black tail that swished constantly against flies. I heard it snort.

The man came through the gate then stopped and looked up. He caught me peeking around the edge of the window. I saw enough to see that he was not a scholar. He made a small bow in my direction, touched the mezuzah and kissed his fingers and then knocked on the door of the inn. I waited and made Babette come upstairs to get me.

'Marta my dear, he's here.'

She was emotional, I wasn't. I was flat as a matzoh. And I would have done anything anyone asked of me if I could have avoided going downstairs. Walking down those stairs – I was descending into a chasm of the unknown and undesired.

Here are my initial impressions of David Ferd Soykher: His smell was so sour that my eyes watered when we were introduced. Because of this I could tell that Babette thought I was taken with him. He's taller than he looked beside the horse. He has a big chest and big arms and a long dark bearded face, weathered and cracked. His hands are thick and look permanently dirty especially around the nails and in the creases. He has a look to him as though he can't quite figure something out.

There was some meaningless conversation with the four of us then Babette saw us off at the door. We were going for our little walk – the nice couple. I had nothing to say to him so I was silent. He finally decided to go ahead and ask me a question.

'Nice weather, huh?'

This from a man who wants me to marry him?

'Yes, it's lovely out.'

We walked up the hill which is a direction I seldom travel. I saw a few people out and several women stood in their doorways and took note. This will be big news in Jebenhausen... the whore is walking out with David Ferd Soykher.

I felt his discomfort when I was quiet but I had

no intention of making it easy for him. He might as well know from the beginning that I'm not interested. Then that man surprised me even more.

'I've seen you, Miss Lindauer... Marta. You are a strong woman and that's what I need. I have four small motherless children at home as well as a hearth to be tended. My old mother lives there and you can bring yours, as well. I'm honest in my dealings and have every intention, God willing, to provide for you until death parts us. Your mother has given her blessing, so... will you marry me and be my wife?'

I could tell that he thought he had made me an offer of riches beyond compare. Four children! Gott im Himmel. I didn't need to ask why his wife died... he wore her out. And just like that I was supposed to say yes and take care of his four children and his mother and mine?

I looked directly at his face and into his eyes but he wouldn't look at me. His skin was dirty and his eyes looked everywhere but at me. I was thinking: if he really wants to marry me shouldn't he look at me?

It was hard to believe that he had truly asked me to marry him not even ten minutes after we met. What was I supposed to say? I know him not at all this David Ferd Soykher. He could be kind or he might be wicked. I wondered what his reaction would be when I said no. I also didn't want to waste my time or his effort in being courted. I guess he didn't want to either.

I turned us around and headed back down the hill. With all my might I couldn't come up with the right way to say it so I put him off.

'Reb Ferd Soykher, please forgive me but I'll need a little time. I'll give you an answer in three days... on Thursday. Marriage is something to be taken seriously...'

He interrupted me.

'Oh, I'm serious, alright. You're just the girl I'm looking for.'

Then his eyes went to my bodice and he made a kind of grimace. It wasn't a smile but whatever it was it sent a shudder through me. I heard the word 'NO' being shouted over and over in my head. I wanted to be far away from that man.

We returned to the inn where his big horse stood waiting. For a moment, I considered his offer just so I could be around such beautiful horses. Then, I said goodbye.

When I went inside here's what happened:

Mother: Well...?

Me: Well what?

Mother: Don't give me your lip. What happened?

Me: He asked me to marry him.

Here she threw up her hands and praised the Lord. She clapped and stomped around but I couldn't understand why she was so happy.

Me: Why are you so happy about this? If I marry him it means that I'll have to leave the inn you know.

Mother: What do you mean if? Do you think I want to continue to do all this work for the rest of my life? Did it ever occur to you that I might want to be done with this place of horrid memories? No of course not, you're too selfish to think of that...

She said more things like this. Once she starts it's not easy to turn her off. Then she pulled out her supreme weapon.

Mother: Shame on you... you've brought nothing but shame on this house. The least you can do is marry this man and get me out of here. I've had it with this place. I'm ready to sit in my chair like the old woman that I am. God knows I've earned it.

There was plenty that I wanted to say but I held my tongue. As I said before she makes me sick. A daughter should want what her mother wants for her but in our case this isn't true.

She fixed her haughty stance then asked me outright, with that mean sneer in her voice, 'What did you say to him?'

I told her what I had told Ferd Soykher. You can imagine her response. I was shaking in my shoes but I stood there until she had worn herself out on me then I got busy.

I'm doomed. I don't know how to do what I have to do. Even if that man was someone I would consider, I wouldn't consider him even then. All day long I've felt myself sliding down down down. Tonight I'm trying to think of a reason to even stay alive. Nothing's right, nothing can ever be right. Why keep on living? Is this God's gift of life to me? Is this what it's supposed to feel like?

19 Av, 5549
August 11, 1789

I get so tired of wandering in the dark. Two days from now I must tell David Ferd Soykher that I won't marry him. In a way it'll be easy. But in another it means the sky will fall and... I don't know what else. It doesn't matter anyway... nothing does.

I did go to see Babette early this morning. She was concerned that I was feeling so low. I told her again that I don't want to marry the man and of course she tried every way she could think of to convince me that I should go ahead and do it.

She said to me, 'Smart smart smart... but you are not so smart.' She's certain that my life will improve once I'm not running the inn any more.

My problem is that I don't have a good reason for not wanting to marry. Well I do have a good reason but no one else thinks it's a good enough reason. They think I should let the past stay in the past. But how do I do that when my past lives in me now? If anyone had any idea how bleak the life inside of me feels already they wouldn't make me do this.

I didn't argue with Babette. I just nodded and acted like she was right. How am I going to get out of this? I happen to know that the Talmud specifies that a woman can be acquired as a wife only with her consent and not without it. So I should be able to say no, yes? How can God sanctify a marriage when one of the partners wants no part of it?

I don't feel like writing the story about my

earlier life these days either... everything's all a big icky mess.

20 Av, 5549
August 12, 1789

Now I have one night until doomsday. I worked doubly hard all day to blot out thoughts of what's going to happen tomorrow. I felt like a criminal skulking through the market this morning. I avoided the bookseller and I didn't see Reb Thanhausser either. This day went by so fast I can't even remember what the weather was like.

I swept and scrubbed all the floors top to bottom and washed three cauldrons full of sheets and hung them out. I prepared and served the meals and also cleaned them up and spent some time scraping dried mud off the stoops front and back and then brought in and folded the linens. Now my arms ache and so does my head.

Have I thought about how to tell Reb Ferd Soykher? Yes constantly. I plan to invite him in, sit him down at the table with my mother and just say it... 'Thank you for your offer Reb Ferd Soykher but I cannot accept.' There. That's what I'll say.

I can't imagine what will happen next.

I know I won't sleep tonight but I don't think I can stay up here churning about tomorrow. I'm going out for a walk – the moon's nearly full. I've never done this before... go out at night. Who cares anyway? Who cares at all?

21 Av, 5549
August 13, 1789
early morning

Where to begin? How to tell this unbelievable story?

I got back to my room a couple of hours ago and after all that happened I thought I would never be able to sleep but I did... I fell sound asleep until the rooster crowed.

There's a lot to say but I don't have much time because I'm exhausted and worst of all today's the day I have to do the black deed... in a few hours. I'll write what I can now and finish later tonight after the end of the world has arrived, oy gevalt!

Every sentence I write from now on should have an exclamation mark after it!

When I went out last night I had just stepped into the garden when I caught sight of a man standing by the back gate. I couldn't see who he was and it scared me to death. The figure was silhouetted in the moonlight – one side lit the other in complete shadow. Everything out there had that eerie brightness.

Then the man said, 'Marta?' and I recognized Reb Thanhausser's voice. What was he doing standing there in the moonlight? At our gate?

'Marta? Is that you? I was walking and saw the candle in the window. I thought it must be yours.'

The gentleness of his voice....

'Yes it's me. I couldn't sleep. I've been writing.'

I walked over to where he stood and he opened the gate and ushered me through. I could see him plainly in the moonlight but he and everything around us looked different because there were no colors – just greys and black.

He looked at me with such tenderness that I was embarrassed – I couldn't talk. Then he put his arm on my shoulder and turned me and we started walking up the path together. The trees and rocks, even the grasses had big shadows because of how bright it was out there. I liked it and I liked walking with him... it felt easy. Neither of us said anything for a few minutes. Then he finally spoke up:

'What were you writing about on this beautiful night, Marta? Something was keeping you awake...'

I tried to decide if I wanted to tell him about my meeting with Reb Ferd Soykher and worse, about the fact that he had asked me to marry him. And my conclusion was that so far in my life Reb Thanhausser had always been kind and reasonable with me so it would be all right to tell him.

'Well yes something rather large was keeping me up, something I wish I didn't have to think about at all.'

'Oh? Do you want to tell me about it?'

No no no no no. I did not want to. I wanted the whole thing to go away.

'Um, well... Babette has brokered an offer of marriage for me.'

He stopped where he was and turned toward me. And I was so surprised by his expression which was astonishment and horror. I do believe that the shadows of the night made him look more distraught than he might have in daylight but I couldn't disagree with his reaction. It took him a moment to respond.

'Who? Who is it, Marta?' He sounded serious.

'His name is Reb Ferd Soykher. He's a horse dealer from Ulm. He came two days ago and asked me to be his wife.' There was no happiness in my words. 'I told him I would give him my answer tomorrow or maybe it's later today by now.'

I looked off across the valley and watched clouds fly over the moon. The light moved and shifted across the land. In the distance, on the horizon, I saw lightning and we heard the sound of faint thunder. It was strange out there – a quiet ghostly world. I forgot that I wasn't alone but his voice brought me back.

'Marta, are you going to marry this man?'

Even in that peculiar light I saw that his eyes were filled with tears.

'Oh no, I never had any intention of marrying him. I don't ever want to be married period... to anyone.' I probably sounded too light-hearted but that was an easy answer for me.

Reb Thanhausser dabbed at his eyes with his handkerchief and looked up to the heavens the way he does. I couldn't take my eyes off him. He seemed so handsome and so sincere.

The wind picked up a little then he spoke gently.

'Dearest girl. You say you want never to marry

but do you have that choice? What about your mother? Will she allow you to say no?'

I was stricken.

'You're right. She won't... I'm sure she won't. She and Babette cooked this up and you can be certain they're not going to let my desires have any bearing on the decision.' I knew just then that it was really true.

That rushing downward feeling started in me. I was being sucked under again in front of Reb Thanhausser. Believe me when I say I did not know what to do. He could tell something was going on in me.

'My dearest Marta, you mean so much to me. The idea of you becoming another man's wife sounds as dreadful to me as it must to you. I don't want to see you unhappy in any way, ever.'

He put his hands on my shoulders, looked right into my eyes and then:

'If it's true that you do not want to marry ever, then I will respect your wish. But, would you consider another proposal? One from someone who knows you and believes you to be a young woman of greatness?'

I stood on a knife's edge once again... many

hideous voices and faces threatened from the edges.

'So,' he continued, 'I know this is not the way it is usually done... I mean, without a shadchan and all of the rituals surrounding engagement and marriage. But what is usual about your life, or mine for that matter? All of these feelings that we have had passing between us? They have led me to love you. I love you Marta, fully and unconditionally. I want to share my life with you and love you and keep you safe in my arms until we are gone from this earth.'

He dropped down on one knee and held my hands.

'I want to be with you... forever. I love you... more than anyone else I have ever known. Can't you see it? We are bashert – meant to be together. From the first time I saw you, when you were a little girl, I knew we had a special bond. And now, now that I've found you again I don't want to lose you... ever. Marta my dearest... please join with me and be my wife. I will love you and protect you forever... my darling.'

I was stunned beyond speech. I was stunned to my core. Marry Reb Thanhausser? Be Reb Thanhausser's wife? But that would mean that we would have to...

I could not fathom such a thing.

While I was reeling from his proposal he remained on one knee, shaking with emotion, dabbing his eyes and looking into mine with such intensity that I had to look away. I was completely unprepared – I didn't know what to say or do. I said nothing.

He stood up then and put his arm gently around my shoulder and I let him. Somehow time moved slower up there on the mountainside and we stood for a long time like that. When we were both calmed he talked some more.

'Marta, do you have anyone else in your life who cares for you as I do?'

Well he knew the answer to that before he asked it.

'Reb Thanhausser, I...'

'Please Marta, my name is Ascher... call me Ascher.'

'That won't be easy for me but I'll try. Ascher (it sounded so strange when I said it) you're the kindest most caring person in my life. There's no one else I can talk to the way we talk. You have always listened to me and helped me.'

But did that mean we should get married? I really didn't understand why I had to be a wife... anyone's wife.

As for the parts about sharing his life and being safe in his arms, I could imagine those. But it was the man-woman covenant that I knew I couldn't abide. Besides, I thought it would probably be important for me to love him back the way he said he loved me and just then I didn't feel such a strong love for him. I like him, I care for him and I do have a measure of what might be love for him. But with his feelings displayed so strongly, I recoiled. Even though he's different from any man I've ever met he's still a man.

'Reb Thanhausser... Ascher... I, I don't know what to say.' I could barely talk. 'You're such a good man. I remember when I was small, how nice you were to me... how you kept my secret for so long... how...'

Then I broke down. Feelings rushed in, feelings rushed out... I blubbered and sobbed. Large scabs from wounds deep inside broke loose and got cried out of me. And Ascher, still quite strange to say, held me in his arms and soothed me and comforted me. I heard him say something about having wanted to do that for a long time and I must admit it did feel nice. I don't ever remember someone holding me like that... not ever.

When I finally could I told him the truth. 'You don't want me. I'm a broken mess. I'm black inside... empty and ugly. No man will want me once he knows me. You should run away as fast as you can. Find a wife who is a good woman, not the evil person that I am...'

I think I may have been shouting because when I was done my voice was hoarse and my throat was a little sore. Reb Thanhausser, I mean Ascher, shook me softly by the shoulders.

'Marta... Dear, dear Marta. You may believe those things about yourself but I know you better than that. You are beautiful inside and out. You are not evil...'

'Oh yes, Reb Tha.. Ascher. I am. I live in me. I know.'

I could see his face in the moonlight and he looked good... familiar.

'Marta, listen to me. For many years I have wondered why God drew us together when you were little and now I know. It was not because Samuel needed me – it was for you, my darling. I remember well what a smart and gifted child you were, and those things don't change in a person no matter how difficult your circumstances may have been growing up after I left. Whatever blackness you feel is in you, that is not who you really are. It's only because of what happened to you. I know that.'

Then before I had a chance to think or even talk he leaned forward and kissed me directly on my mouth. How warm his lips felt, how soft. A huge thrill ran through me. Up close he smelled good, too.

What did he do then? Did he run away like I had suggested? No. He took my hand and pulled me along farther up the path.

'Let's go to Heaven, Marta. My guess is that it's beautiful in there tonight. Let's go see, eh?'

What could I do? We weren't far from the place and I liked being out on the mountain in the middle of the night... with him... an adventure in an exotic land.

Neither of us said anything as we walked but I was excited. Once I stumbled and he threw his arm around me and helped me stay upright. Such a strong sure presence he was.

Just as we arrived at the entrance to Heaven the wind picked up and the air smelled like rain close by. We were too far from the inn to run back before it hit so we decided to go into Heaven and find shelter there. We both ran straight to the slash in the big beech and luckily, moments after we backed ourselves in, the heavens opened up.

There we were squeezed together with our knees drawn up in a dark and noisy rainstorm but we were safe and dry inside. We had room to sit up beside each other... I didn't mind.

Reb Thanhausser felt like my brother. Not Samuel but a different brother... someone else who I could be myself with. We snuggled close and sat listening to the rain. He persisted with his request.

'What do you say Marta? Will you marry Ferd Soykher or spend the rest of your life with a man who loves you with all his heart? Hmmm?'

I decided to tell him straight out.

'Ascher, I cannot be with a man, not in the way that a wife is commanded by God to be. That's the truth. I can't do it.'

Although I couldn't see him I could tell he was thinking. The rain fell around us in the glade but we were dry inside the tree.

'It is important that you understand what I'm going to say to you, Marta.' He took ahold of my hand. 'My desire to be with you is not predicated on the fulfillment of that particular portion of God's commandment. I have a strong yearning to protect you and provide you with the kind of love that you have never received, or rather that you haven't felt since Samuel died. I know how he loved you. And I love you too, equally. Do you understand what I'm telling you?'

'Do you mean we wouldn't have to do that? Ever?'

'We don't know what the future will bring, nor do we know how our love may grow. In time, you may come to accept me as a man, but I would be grateful to God if only you would accept my wish to marry you so that we may spend the rest of our days together.'

'What if I don't love you enough Ascher? What if you come to see for yourself what a vile and horrible person I really am? You'll be sorry and I'll ruin everything.'

He chuckled a little.

'My dear, why don't we learn together who it is who truly dwells within your soul? I am a good judge of human character. When I look at you I see a beautiful jewel whom God has placed in my life for a reason.'

I felt small as a flea. I didn't want to commit to him or any man but he was right. My mother was not going to dismiss Ferd Soykher's proposal as easily as I had. She would probably not dismiss it at all. She would force me to marry that large coarse horse trader and I would end up invisible in a life that was worse, much worse, than the one I was already in.

The more I thought about it the surer I was that I would have no say about it – I had to respond.

'Well if there's no other alternative and if my choice is between Ferd Soykher and you Ascher, then I... I... choose you.' It wasn't easy to say but I said it.

Yes he was happy. He kissed my hand, squeezed it, put his arm around me and sent a prayer of thanks to God.

'You will never be sorry for this Marta, I promise.'

I felt sick for having gone against my own vow to myself never to marry, but also relief. If I had to do it, at least I would be with someone who loved me. Perhaps I could learn to love him more. How I would ever break the news to my mother was the big question.

I don't have anyone to tell any of this to except

for you, Fraynd. What if I didn't have my pen and paper? It's a dreadful thought. It would be as though I never even existed.

What happened next was the most unexpected thing that has ever happened in my life. We were cramped in there so we moved around a little trying to get more comfortable. I felt him reach one arm up above his head. He said he wanted to see how high the cavity went which I would never have done... crawling creatures and such.

'Marta, there is something here!'

We adjusted ourselves so he could get both arms up and he felt around some more.

'It is a bundle, wrapped in leather. There is something resting in a cleft above us!'

My skin prickled when he said that. I thought Samuel and Ascher and I were the only ones who knew about Heaven. Did bandits go there too? Was it a stash of treasure? A dead body?

When Ascher was struggling to pull whatever it was down, a spray of rotten dead wood fell on me. I imagined giant beetles and spiders and brushed it off then pulled my shawl up over my head and bent over to protect my face from more of it. I could hear him struggling to free whatever it was. The whole time he was describing what he was doing:

'It is a large object... I am trying to ease it out... I do not want to break it... what could it be?...' And so on like that.

I scrunched way over to one side to give him more room and then he got on his knees. I could tell from the sounds he was making that it wasn't easy to get it loose. A couple of times he had to stop to spit stuff out of his mouth.

When the bundle was finally freed he maneuvered it around until it sat across both our laps. In the darkness he ran his hands over and around it looking for a way to get it open. He kept saying 'What could it be?'

The moment I felt the weight and shape of it myself I had a schreck like I have never ever felt before. I remembered Samuel on his deathbed when he leaned over to me just before he died. What did he say? He said 'Heaven.' I realized just then that he had been saying 'Marta, I saved it for you and it's in Heaven'. Not... I'm going to heaven, but... 'your treasure is in our Heaven... now!'

I tried to say something to Ascher because I knew what it was... I knew! But I was overcome and couldn't talk.

And it didn't take him long to figure out what I was crying about. He recognized the shape of the violin case in the dark even wrapped in that thick leather skin. He put his arm around my shoulder and I held on to that thing and cried and cried and cried.

Once I was recovered enough to talk again we decided to replace the violin in its hiding place until we could return together to retrieve it in the daylight and look at it – later today, this afternoon. Then we made our way back to town in the drizzle of the storm's end hanging onto each other in the dark.

We talked about securing a ketubah, our marriage agreement, which he said he would see to, and when we should have our wedding. Problems arose immediately though because we both knew that my mother would never agree to our union. She had no love for Reb Thanhausser and had already made her arrangement for me with Ferd Soykher.

If I was honest, I didn't really know how to turn that man down when everything was already in place for us to be engaged. It would bring on the wrath of my mother which I'm not afraid of but I knew I couldn't bear to live with her after defying her that way. I didn't like thinking about the whole thing openly but I had to.

After we talked about it most of the way down the path we came up with a plan. Ascher's idea was for me to accept the man's proposal because that way we would have time during the engagement to figure out how to proceed together. It would be a big deception for sure but we had a laugh about that. We're both good at keeping a secret and frankly, the more we talked about it, the more I warmed to the idea of being with Ascher as his partner in life. I like him. He's so good. And having his arms around me and being kissed, well... none of it felt bad.

He said not to worry, we would figure out the next step. My only task for the day was to get through the meeting and come out the other side. We hugged and agreed to meet at the back gate in the late afternoon because my precious violin awaits. I can't stop thinking about it up in that tree.

This was a night I will never forget no matter what else ever happens.

Now I must clean up and prepare for a most unpleasant task. I'll be wishing for time to pass in a hurry so I can go back up to Heaven. What a strange life this is. Will this afternoon ever arrive? How will I stand it until then?

21 Av, 5549
August 13, 1789
late night

There is no way for me to write all that has been happening but I will try. First: the meeting with Reb Ferd Soykher.

When I returned from the market, Babette was here sitting at a table with my mother. While I put things away my mother ignored me but she spoke to Babette so I could hear.

'If she knows what's good for her she'll say yes to Ferd Soykher, all right. Little miss perfect thinks she's too good for him but she has another think coming... blah blah blah.'

Babette clucked and said something to try to soothe. I decided to wait and let my mother stew a little longer. She would find out soon enough what my answer was.

When the man arrived, I let him in and offered him a brew and then we all four sat around the table. He did not smell any better than before. I turned my head away from him as much as possible.

Babette was the first one to say something.

'Well Reb Ferd Soykher, we know that you're

anxious to hear what Marta's answer will be.'

He nodded.

'Yes, ma'am.' He looked (leered) at me. I expected him to drool next. 'She's a pretty one, a little thin, but with nice strong arms, good teeth, (like he was appraising a horse) and I do want her for my wife... very much.'

He nodded to my mother to acknowledge her approval and then to Babette. All three were exchanging looks. I was irrelevant.

Since no one said anything else, Babette finally initiated the actual dreaded moment.

'Marta dear, Reb Ferd Soykher awaits your decision.'

Against all my better instincts and against many loud voices inside of me, I gave him my answer though I still couldn't look at him. I thought of Ascher and said these words:

'Alright... yes... I will marry you.'

My mother slapped the table, pushed her chair back and gathered three glasses and a bottle of brandy. She poured a shot for each of them and they toasted l'chaim to the grand arrangement. Apparently, I still was not a part of the affair. I couldn't believe what she said next.

'Welcome son, Ferd Soykher. Welcome to the family. This is a wonderful day. I want you two married as soon as we can make arrangements. I say let's shorten the engagement...' here she gave me a wicked look, '...and set a date for next Tuesday.' Then she laughed! She threw her head back and howled like a crazy woman, which she is.

From a far-away place I watched them shake hands and seal the deal. I wasn't breathing, I couldn't talk. All I could think of was Ascher. What would he say, what would he do? I was in big trouble. I started shaking and couldn't stop. They poured another round, lifted their glasses in a toast and threw it back, all three.

I excused myself and ran up to my room but I was too upset to write. That happened early this morning so I had to keep myself busy for hours before I could see Ascher.

Tuesday next! That's five days away... five!

I tried to keep my mind on my work all day, but it was impossible. Tonight, when it was time to slip away to be with Ascher, I checked to make sure she had passed out. And of course, because she had drunk to her happiness and delight so early, I found her snoring at her desk.

When I saw him, I wanted to hug Ascher in broad daylight but I restrained myself. He carried a satchel over his shoulder with a small blanket rolled up in a strap under one arm. I was so glad to see him and couldn't wait to tell him what had happened at the meeting but I held off until we were a ways up the path.

'Ascher, I did it. I agreed to marry David Ferd Soykher. It's done.' That was as much as I could say. When I tried to tell him about the wedding being next Tuesday, I couldn't get the words started.

He stopped so I stopped, and then he looked at me closely.

'What's wrong, Marta? What else happened at the meeting?'

I was grateful for his perception, otherwise I might never have had the courage to tell him the rest. It took strength for me to say what I had to say.

'Well my mother... my loving mother has scheduled our wedding for this coming Tuesday... five days from now.' Stupidly, tears arrived. I have never cried as much as I do these days.

I watched to see what his reaction would be. His tendency is always to think before he acts and that's what he did. He straightened up and shook his head slowly a few times before he said anything. Next he looked directly into my eyes while he stood there thinking, which gave me shivers. Finally he turned and started us walking again up the hill and then he talked.

'This is unfortunate news. We will have to hasten our plans. Come, Marta. Before we do anything else, do you not want to see your violin? I know I do.'

How he could smile at a moment like that, I have no idea. But, yes I did want to get to Heaven and see my violin which I had nearly forgotten about due to another matter.

I ran the last bit and left him behind but he was soon beside me and then we went into Heaven together.

He spread the blanket on the ground near our tree and I knelt down and waited while he retrieved the package. When he laid it there in front of me we were both too awed to touch it.

Imagine – Samuel was the one who saved it. He handled it. He had wrapped it in leather and tied it with rope which was still holding, mostly. Some of the creases in the skin were cracked, some parts of the rope were rotted away. When I couldn't wait any longer I ran my hands around the bundle trying to figure out how to open it. Then, Ascher pulled a knife from his bag and easily cut the cords that held it together.

It took both of us pulling to get the stiff leather to open. And when we finally freed the violin case, he pulled the coverings away and we sat again and gazed at it.

Memories and images flew through my brain. The case looked so familiar. I remembered Samuel's sweet face and, although I didn't like seeing it, a vision of my violin teacher came to me. I felt that strange power he had over me that turned me small and dirty. And then I remembered the feeling of splendor I had when I played my violin... both feelings at once. No wonder I'm such a mess inside. All I really wanted just then was to see my violin.

There was a thin leather strap buckled around the case which I was able to undo, although my hands shook the whole time. I looked at Ascher before I opened it... my friend, my confidant, my future husband. I was glad to be there with him and I told him so with an eager smile which he returned in kind. We were both brimming with anticipation. Yes my heart was pounding.

Then, I unhooked the little rusted latch and used

two hands to carefully lay the top of the case back. The leather hinges were not in bad shape so they held.

The first thing I saw were the hairs from the bow, sprung free from their bindings and littered in a mess over the top of the violin. I gasped in horror because it looked terrible. But Ascher just reached over and gathered them up, lifted the bow stick off and put them all on the blanket.

Then we saw the violin, my beautiful violin. Ascher 'oohed' and you probably know what I did next. I covered my face and cried, but it wasn't only because of seeing it again. It was mainly because the violin was in pieces. The neck was loose from the rest, the top was not attached to the bottom any more, the strings were still knotted to the tailpiece but not to the pegs which had sprung loose and were lying in the bottom of the case along with the bridge. It looked broken and awful. I couldn't imagine how someone would be able to fix a violin when it had come apart like that.

Ascher patted my shoulder until I gathered myself. Neither one of us said anything. When I could bear to look at it again, I saw that the top was all in one piece and the sides were still connected to the back and that was still in one piece, too.

I gently lifted each part with Ascher's help and we laid them out on the blanket. They made a puzzle that fit back together except that they weren't glued. As usual, he knew what to say.

'Well, I do not think you can play it yet, my dear.'

When I looked up at him his eyes were twinkling.

'Oh, Ascher, what do we do now? Who could possibly fix this? *Can it be fixed?*'

I was grateful to have him beside me. He had such a calming manner.

'It looks to me like it's not really broken exactly but has merely come apart at the seams. Look here, don't you agree?'

He turned the top over and we both saw a fine layer of dried glue along the edge. Maybe he was right. Maybe someone could put it back together... but who? I took the top of the violin from his hands and looked at it in a beam of sunlight. Its beautiful colors – browns and yellows and some reds – were the same as I remembered, although it was a bit darker than it had been seven years ago.

'Ascher, what should we do? Do you know someone who can fix it?'

He thought a moment.

'No, but why don't we ask Reb Veberke? He's the one person I can think of in Jebenhausen who might have an idea of where to take it.'

I hated to put my beautiful violin away without playing it but we carefully laid each part back in the case, and after Ascher packed a cloth around the pieces to hold them securely, we closed it.

Then the problem was: how to get it into town without anyone seeing it. I didn't want to wait another minute to get it fixed.

We decided to return the violin to its hiding place for one more night and then we'll both return after sundown on Saturday after Shabbos to collect it and take it to Reb Veberke to look at. So, I said goodbye to my violin again – but not for long.

I reminded Ascher that Tuesday is the day I'm to be married. This thought gives me stomach aches. And then he did something that changed my life and his, forever.

Ascher took my hand as we stood together under the tall pines. He looked into my eyes and I happily looked into his until I felt us merge together – in understanding, in love, in desire.

Yes, I admit I felt desire. I told myself that he

was my true choice for a husband and that those deep feelings moving within me were what a woman feels when she desires her betrothed. I never expected to feel that way, ever. It was a moment of great joy for both of us. Then he said to me:

'Marta, are you ready to become my wife?'

I answered honestly.

'Yes, Ascher. If I could marry you right now, I would.'

Well, the most amazing thing happened. He took a corked bottle from his bag, a small wine glass wrapped in a cloth and also a rolled parchment. And, even though he wore his yarmulke as always, he pulled his prayer shawl over his head.

Then, he turned to me and, with our eyes locked, he lifted my shawl up over my head and wrapped it across my face like a veil. This custom, called badeken, reminds the Jewish people of how Jacob was tricked by Laban into marrying Leah before Rachel, as her face was covered by her veil. So, the groom veils his own wife to make sure she's who he thinks she is, and also so the bride can display her modesty.

In that moment, I realized he really was going to marry me, right there in Heaven, and I was willing.

Ascher said this prayer to me, his bride:

'You, Marta, will be my wife. I will love, cherish and respect the you that is revealed to me and also those parts of you that are hidden from me. In our marriage I will make a space within me that will be filled by you, by only you, for all of our time together.'

I was transfixed, so moved by his kindness and his words. He had planned out the whole thing perfectly. I couldn't believe it was happening.

Next, he unrolled the parchment and showed me our ketubah that he had written out for the two of us. It was beautiful and simple. Then he read it aloud to me.

As he read his vows he promised to protect me, to provide me with food, clothing and support and be my partner in God's covenant. When he got to that part he winked at me and I was ecstatic.

I looked around at the peaceful and precious glen where we stood. Who could ever have a more beautiful and sacred chuppah than ours? The tall pines leaned over us with their ancient benign wisdom and I felt God's presence. We were blessed and holy. Ascher's voice bore its way into my soul where it discovered my happiness.

Next, he poured wine into the glass and after he said the blessing over the wine, and also the betrothal blessing, we both sipped. I couldn't stop looking into his eyes... I was feeling immense love for him. My breast was a flower that was opening toward the sunlight of my beloved. My heart was expanding and exploding.

He took a small plain silver ring from his pocket and laid it in his open palm with this declaration:

'Behold, you are consecrated to me with this ring according to the Law of Moses and Israel.'

Then, he slid the ring onto my finger and it fit! He told me that we should have two witnesses for this but that God wouldn't mind under the circumstances.

I was in another realm – of love and peace – instead of the strife and difficulties of my usual life. Warmth and calmness surrounded us. We were alone together in the world.

Ascher then recited the Sheva Brachot: the Seven Blessings, which I knew marked the end of the ceremony.

But, he faced me and took hold of my hands and recited one more verse from my favorite psalm, Song of Solomon:

'My beloved spoke, and said unto me: Rise up, my love, my fair one, and come away. For, lo, the winter is past, the rain is over and gone. The flowers appear on the earth; the time of singing is come, and the voice of the turtledove is heard in our land. The fig-tree putteth forth her green figs, and the vines in blossom give forth their fragrance. Arise, my love, my fair one, and come away.'

Then, he raised his hands above us, looked down to the ground and said the benediction. 'The Lord bless you and keep you...'

You have to understand that I was completely carried away.

After he stomped and shattered the glass in the cloth, he kissed me. I felt warmth and protection flood through me. Now, I was his wife and he, my husband. Our only witnesses were God, the trees and the woodland fairies.

We kissed until he lowered me onto the blanket and then we kissed lots more. I had no unease about what I was doing. All I knew was I wanted it, I wanted him and I didn't want to stop. I had no idea that I would enjoy being so familiar with him.

Before long we both decided that we had too many clothes on so, in that sweet warm haven, we tenderly removed each other's garments. I was left with just my shift and he, beautiful he, wore nothing.

Let it be known that we did, indeed, consummate our marriage and that I, Marta Lindauer Thanhausser, found delight and happiness with my new husband, Ascher Thanhausser. It all felt right, none of it felt wrong.

Yes, I had some moments where fear rose up sharp and uninvited. But my beloved and I talked and loved our way through the fear each time and back into love. What a gift from God is love. What a gift is my husband, Ascher. I am the luckiest woman on earth.

We walked down the mountain path together as husband and wife and the world looked different to me... livelier, more colorful. Now I understood the true reason for celebrating a marriage. I wanted to sing and dance and let all of creation know how happy I was. But of course, I couldn't do any of that because my life is still confined by deception and potential disaster.

Ascher left me at the back gate with these words:

'My wife. I am yours and you are mine. We will find a way to be together soon, Marta... Marta Thanhausser. Meet me here after sundown on

Saturday. By then I will have a plan so that you will not have to marry twice! And, we can get your violin repaired and be together. Until then, my love... the hours will pass far too slowly... Shabbos Shalom.'

I had to get inside to prepare the evening meal and I didn't want him to leave. He watched me remove my wedding ring and hide it in the small pocket of my skirt. Then, we parted with no display of affection, a difficult and unwelcome task.

So, dear Fraynd, I am a married woman! And, a happy one. I can't ever remember feeling this happy, ever. I'm so grateful for this day.

23 Av, 5549
August 15, 1789
early evening

I'm wondering why I don't feel bad about this deception. I should be in my dark place waiting for the end of the world to arrive but instead I feel like skipping around. I can't stop thinking about being with Ascher in Heaven. The scenes play over and over in my mind: the sound of his voice, his delicious scent, our wedding, our loving, my violin... And, all of these memories make me happy, not glum.

I'm also having some evil enjoyment knowing that my mother is fooled once again and there's nothing she can do about it. It's now Saturday night after Shabbos and the candle is nearly burned down. The inn is quiet. I'm going to meet Ascher in a few minutes, but I wanted to write first.

My mother told me that Hindel will be arriving late tomorrow to help with preparations for my wedding to David Ferd Soykher. Ha! Won't they be surprised when they find out I'm already married to Ascher Thanhausser. I've tried to imagine how it might go when I tell but so far I haven't figured out what exactly I should say. Maybe I'll just blurt it out and see what happens. Oy vey.

I can't wait to see Ascher again and I'm excited to take my violin to Reb Veberke. I wonder what Ascher's plan will be. I hope someone will be able to repair my violin. I'm going crazy. I'll write more later.

23 Av, 5549
August 15, 1789
late night

Here's a story for you, Fraynd. I'm shaking with excitement as I write this.

Ascher met me at the back gate with the violin. He went out as soon as it was dark enough and collected it then he picked me up and we walked to Reb Veberke's. He invited us in and, with candlestick in hand, led us through the quiet shop into his home, a cozy apartment of one room with a striped cat sleeping on the bed. There were two chairs which Ascher and I sat on. Reb Veberke sat on the corner of the bed and I reached over and petted the kitty.

On the wall behind him was another of those textured weavings, like the one he showed me before. This one was smaller but just as beautiful, with layers of rich colors: purple, dark green, dark blue, some pink and other beiges and grays that looked like a scene from a faraway make-believe land when I squinted my eyes at it in the candlelight.

The first thing Ascher did was he showed Reb Veberke the ketubah and told him that we were husband and wife in the eyes of God. Before he said a word Reb Veberke took three glasses and a jug off the shelf. After he had poured for each of us, he made a toast to the newlyweds, 'Mazel Tov'. He gave us a warm smile and downed his draught. Ascher and I did the same. So, Reb Veberke was happy for us.

He listened as we told him about our wedding in

Heaven. He offered to sign the ketubah as a proxy witness, which they both laughed at. Then, Ascher took him up on it.

While they saw to that I looked around the room. Reb Veberke didn't have much – a few dishes and drinking glasses, a pair of worn smooth wooden candlesticks, some clothing hung on hooks, a bowl for the cat on the floor.

But, next to his bed, he had a shelf with thirteen books on it. I also saw some sheets of paper lying on the table which had sketches of trees and people on them. They were striking likenesses, and looking at them stirred something in me... desire... impatience... they made me want to draw or write or, most of all, play music on my violin.

Reb Veberke was curious about the violin case which Ascher had put on the bed so we opened it and laid the pieces out on the quilt. Reb Veberke moved the candle back and forth over them while we told him all about how Samuel had wrapped it up in leather and stashed it in the tree seven years ago. I told him how Samuel had tried to tell me about it with his very last breath but that I had misunderstood.

The moment I told him that a big sob rolled up through me and I was overcome... bawling in front of both men.

While I fumbled like an idiot for a cloth in my pocket, I saw my violin on the bed which gave me two opposing thoughts at the same time: a beautiful thing, a broken thing. I couldn't make sense of any of it. I was caught in a bad daydream, all weepy and stupid.

But, I kept hearing Ascher's kind soft voice talking to me and that calmed me down. In a minute I felt less moronic and not so embarrassed... more innocent than just plain wrong. When I had finally wiped my nose and face enough, I looked up.

Both men were still sitting quietly in Reb Veberke's room. Nothing had changed. They were being their kind and quiet selves while I had been lost in a storm. Ascher smiled and nodded at me then squeezed my hand as we watched Reb Veberke lift the violin's top and hold it near the flame.

'In all my days, and may I have many more God willing, I have rarely seen anything as fine and delicate as this violin.' He hefted the carved wooden top piece a few times. 'It feels inconsequential, almost too light to carry out the occupation for which it was designed.'

Ascher answered, 'I remember well Veberke, how this instrument sounded when it was assembled. And, you can be sure that what flowed forth from these few pieces of wood was reminiscent of angels singing, particularly when Marta's touch was applied.'

Reb Veberke turned toward me. 'But you were just a child Marta, isn't that so?' I nodded. 'Well, then you have a gift from God... that's all there is to it.'

Ascher looked at me with love in his eyes. 'She does, indeed. My Marta is a gem with many facets...'

They both found it necessary to direct their gaze at me without pause which made me uncomfortable. I am only me and no gemstone. A dull stone is more like it.

I felt my insides falling down through me. I wanted to disappear. I'm not used to such straightforward affection, not in front of anyone, especially another man even if he was Reb Veberke.

'... she is my beautiful wife, and I thank the Holy One with every breath for bringing us together.'

All I could do was put my head down. My cheeks turned hot.

Reb Veberke jumped in to change the subject. 'Have you been writing in your little booklet Marta? The one you showed me?'

I was grateful for a different topic so I told him about my writing, mainly how much I love to write my daily entries. I didn't tell him that I was nearly out of paper because there has been so much to write about and my ink was running dry. I've had to add drops of water so I can keep going which makes the words lighter and lighter on the paper.

Then, he tapped his head with his finger to show us that he had a good idea. He went to a cupboard that stood against the wall near his table and pulled out four large curling sheets of paper. He rolled them and tied them with a piece of yarn and then he handed them to me with a noble bow. Next, he reached into the cupboard again and pulled out a small jar of ink, nearly full, and handed that to me, as well.

'For your wedding, my dear. May you write forevermore, God willing... or...' he winked at me, '...at least while this paper lasts.'

I couldn't believe he had given me such a wonderful gift. Ascher's eyes were shining. I couldn't say a word... too much feeling alive in me. But I pulled myself together the best I could and thanked him.

'You may not understand Reb Veberke, what this gift means to me. I was almost out of ink and paper. How can I ever thank you enough?'

'Listen, Marta. When God put you together he did everything right. He bestowed many gifts on you...'

He continued to talk like this but of course, my busy thoughts reminded me that as nice as those comments from him felt, he didn't really know what he was saying.

Only a small part of me accepted his words, the rest of me thought him foolish and ignorant. Well, I'm actually the foolish and ignorant one. What is special about me... who lies, who deceives, who is ugly, and filled with anger and hatred toward my mother? Why would Ascher want me when there is so much wrong with me?

Ascher jolted me out of my thinking gulley. He took hold of my hand and that brought me back to Reb Veberke's room, away from my thoughts. In my mind everything was dark and bleak. But, in Reb Veberke's room life felt warm and hopeful... and safe.

'Veberke, we need a plan in order to announce our marriage to Marta's mother and the town. We also need to find someone who can make Marta's violin new again.'

No matter how I thought about it, I couldn't imagine telling my mother that I had married Reb Thanhausser. I couldn't picture myself saying those words to her under any conditions.

Ascher continued, 'I have given this considerable contemplation and before I can fashion a strategy I have to ask you this, Veberke. Do you know of someone nearby who can fix this violin? I must put this instrument back into Marta's hands.'

Reb Veberke squinted an eye at me as he thought about it.

'There's no one in Jebenhausen who makes or repairs violins. The label on this violin says it was made seven years ago in Nuremberg so I suppose the maker lives there yet. However, the city is many days' walk from here and no Jew is allowed to enter unless he is willing to pay an exorbitant fee and be escorted by an armed soldier. Am I correct in assuming you may not want to go that route?' He directed this to Ascher.

'You are correct, sir. I do have some savings after serving as the teacher at the school these past seven years. But, I do not have enough to give any of it away to tax collectors.' He made a bad face.

Reb Veberke and I both laughed a little.

'No, I don't suppose you do. Well...' he rubbed his chin whiskers, 'you will have to travel to make this happen, Thanhausser. Are you prepared to do that? Now that you're married, albeit clandestinely, it looks like some big changes may be in order for you and Marta.'

I watched Ascher as he prepared his answer. He looked at me to see what my response might be.

The idea of leaving Jebenhausen and making a journey was a surprise to me. I've always known that traveling is dangerous – I've never had a desire to go anywhere away from Jebenhausen. I would have to leave my home and my mother... an interesting idea. But, if that was what we needed to do in order to get my violin repaired then I was willing.

I swallowed down hard and nodded yes to Ascher. Then he turned to Reb Veberke and bobbed his head once. Reb Veberke told us this:

'Alright. Here's what I know. There are many violinmakers living and working in Markneukirken, east of here near the Czech border. It would be a long trek...'

Ascher interrupted: 'Yes, I know the place. It's not far from where I grew up, actually. But, I'm not of a mind to have us travel east. My inclination is to head west, toward possibilities that lie in that direction.'

The two men paused in their conversation and looked at each other. Reb Veberke raised an eyebrow.

'America?'

My insides clenched. I watched Ascher. He hunched his shoulders and put a little grin on his face.

'Maybe. Maybe not. We'll see....'

He looked right at me and we nodded yes to each other. My life was going in an astounding direction.

Reb Veberke continued: 'The other center of violinmaking in Germany is in Mittenwald... south of here just before the Alps, near Austria. It too is many days away.'

The room became silent as both men thought about all of this. I petted the kitty and wondered where in the world we would be going.

They talked a bit about what the route to Mittenwald might require then Reb Veberke tapped his head like before when he remembered something. Here's what he said:

'I was in Stuttgart several years ago and while I was there I passed by a luthier shop. I remember the name on the sign because I thought it unusual to have a French violinmaker working in that city... the name was Lupot. If he's still there, I dare say that would be your closest option. It's only about 35 kilometers. You could walk it in two or three days to be sure.'

I have heard about Stuttgart all my life but never imagined I would travel back there for any reason. Thinking about it I got a little excited but it also gave me an upset stomach.

Ascher answered, 'If there's a possibility that we could get this instrument repaired in Stuttgart then I think we should go there, Marta.' He took ahold of my hands which I was glad about because I had started shaking again. 'This goes along with my earlier plan of how to break the news to your mother and the town.'

I shook more when he said that. When he saw the look on my face he cupped my cheek with his hand. 'Marta, you have nothing to worry about. You're married to me now. I will protect you from whatever offensive insults that woman throws your way.'

That made me blurt out: 'Ascher, you already

told me that you don't ever want to see or speak to my mother again. So, how do you expect to protect me from her wrath if you're not even there when I tell her?'

For a moment, I had forgotten where we were and that Reb Veberke was listening to us. Then, he interrupted.

'Thanhausser, what exactly is your plan to extricate you and Marta from her mother and the rest of this town. You're a salaried employee of Jebenhausen. You can't just up and leave, can you?'

I really wanted to hear his response. Ascher sat for nearly a minute thinking through his answer. While he thought, I tried to calm my insides although it wasn't easy.

'My idea is similar to yours, Veberke. I think Marta and I should leave Jebenhausen as soon as possible. You understand that she's scheduled to marry the horse dealer David Ferd Soykher on Tuesday? This is Saturday, almost Sunday, so we must act quickly in order to avoid a disagreeable confrontation with the man.'

I had to barge in. 'Ascher don't you see? It will be more than just a disagreeable confrontation with my mother when I tell her I'm leaving. It will be the end of the world. I don't ever want to do it. I would rather sneak away while she's asleep and never see her again.'

The room got quiet as the echo of my words slowly faded. The men looked at each other and then at me. They both had a serious look on their face.

'Marta,' Ascher turned to me, 'I am willing to face your mother in order to be there with you when we tell her. I don't want you to have to do it alone. Do you understand? We can do it together.'

I kept seeing a vision of my mother screaming at me and throwing things. For me, deception has always worked better than telling her the truth about anything.

'Please Ascher... Reb Veberke... I don't want to have this confrontation with her. It's too big of a breach. She'll go nuts.'

Reb Veberke: Will it matter how awfully she behaves if it means you get to leave?

Me: When she screams at me like that something wild in me switches on. My heart pounds, my breathing gets heavy and I just want to attack her with claws. I don't know if I could control myself even with you standing beside me, Ascher. She hates you, you know.

Neither one said anything so I kept going. 'I would rather pack up my writing book and a few other things and run away with you in the middle of the night than ever face her again. Let her wake up to find me gone. That would be what she deserves anyway for forcing me to marry that awful Ferd Soykher. She's never cared about me. She's only interested in getting herself out of the inn and having me be her personal slave forever.'

I stopped when I realized that I was ranting and raving like she does. I had to remove my shawl I was so heated up.

Ascher sat for a long time thinking. Reb Veberke said nothing. He petted the cat. Finally Ascher spoke:

'As much as I dislike the idea of stealing away from Jebenhausen under cover of darkness I can see the benefit of making our exit in such a manner for your sake, Marta. Because of that here's what I propose we do: I will speak with Elias Gutmann tomorrow and explain to him that I've been called away. I may tell him the real reason for my sudden departure and also that we're married but I will have to make that determination during our conversation.'

'You must make your own preparations for our

leave-taking, Marta. We will set out for Stuttgart tomorrow late, after the town has settled for the night.'

He paused to see my reaction but I couldn't even move. What if we're accosted by bandits in the night? What if we lose our way? Fear and excitement mixed up inside me but overall I summoned bravery. Why not set off on an adventure? It would be better than staying one day longer at the Lindauer inn. I nodded my answer: Yes. I didn't hear any other voices in me saying No.

Reb Veberke spoke up. 'I'm not keen on your idea of walking that road at night, Thanhausser. The moon is heading toward dark... there are brigands at large. Do you know the route? Why don't you wait until Monday morning so you can lease a ride on a cart going in your direction?'

When he put it that way I agreed with Reb Veberke. Nighttime travel sounded too scary. But, Ascher explained himself.

'Yes I understand, Veberke. There are lowlifes about but we can use caution and stealth and I am familiar with the route – I traveled to Stuttgart two years ago for a meeting. It will be important for us to get as far away from Jebenhausen as we can tomorrow night so that Madam Lindauer has no recourse but to tolerate her daughter's disappearance. Remember, she won't know in which direction we will have traveled. We will only need to make use of the night's darkness once. After that we can seek shelter en route. And once we're in Stuttgart we can surely find lodging in the Jewish quarter.'

I was to leave Jebenhausen with Ascher Thanhausser, who is my own husband! The more I thought about it the more I was ready to go.

We ended our conversation with Reb Veberke by deciding that Ascher would secretly make all necessary arrangements with the officials in town tomorrow. And my job will be to prepare myself for the biggest change of my entire life in one day!

We put the wrapped pieces of my violin back in the case and secured it with the strap. Then we said our good-byes to our friend and I did remember to thank him for the miraculous gifts.

At the inn, Ascher and I embraced madly and then he took the violin home with him. I returned to my garret where I now sit writing by candlelight on the last night of my stay in this cauldron of memories.

How will I ever make it through the day tomorrow knowing that it is to be my last?

Knowing that with the night will come my escape from this detestable existence...

Sleep tonight? Ha!

24 Av 5549
August 16, 1789

This will be my last entry in my book in this part of my life and I don't know when I'll be able to write again or what will happen to me before I do.

I spent the day cleaning the inn for my wedding that is supposed to happen the day after tomorrow. A wall has gone up in front of my life here and behind it is my new life that starts as soon as I walk out the door in a little while.

My sister arrived this afternoon along with her husband and three small children. They're staying in the big room on the second floor. The baby is only seven months old. She cried all evening just to add to the high pitch already going inside my head.

Hindel greeted me with her usual superiority. It's been months since I've seen her yet my feelings for her were exactly the same as ever. I love her but I can't stand her. She's bossy and always right. She immediately started ordering me around like time had not passed and she was still in charge of me. I had generosity to spare because I won't ever see her again after tonight.

It's not easy to grasp such an idea but all day long I looked at things and people around me with new eyes. I was a step back from their lives and none of it meant anything to me... the inn or the people. I was dead in my old life, no longer interested in any of them.

Hope wrapped her arms around me and carried me aloft through the hours. All day long a vision of Ascher's face floated by my side and that, along with the promise of playing my violin again soon, has delivered me to the moment of my leave taking which will be in a few minutes.

I also admit to a constant low current of spiced nerves under my skin that kept me trembling all day and has me trembling still. I made myself not think about all the dangers out there in the world.

Everything I want to take is packed into the valise that has sat unused forever under the stairs: a few clothes, my shawl, my hairbrush, my papers. I made a new book with the paper from Reb Veberke, and brought that and my ink jar wrapped tightly in cloth so it shouldn't leak, my quills, a few small necessary items and that's all.

I'm not happy about leaving behind my collection

of beautiful stones so I'm bringing my three favorites with me. I plan to stop in the kitchen on the way out to leave a note and to find some food to take with us.

Babette came by this morning to check on preparations for the wedding. She and my mother are travelling in a completely different direction from me. I tried to be agreeable with both of them mainly for my own safety in getting out of here. I'm sure I left no clues as to my plans so won't they be surprised tomorrow when I'm not here!

Even though I feel that deep down inside I'm a good person, one wouldn't know it from my devious behavior.

Hindel's baby cries without pause – you would think she'd run down. As soon as that baby quiets and the rest of the house settles, I'm leaving.

I'll write my last thoughts to you, Fraynd. You have listened patiently to my small problems and complaints. You have made my life feel bigger and more important than it really is. I'm grateful to have you and grateful to have Ascher Thanhausser by my side for the rest of my life. I can't believe it... Ascher loves me. How will I ever be able to make him understand what his love means to me? How will I ever love him enough?

This is what I wrote in the note that I will leave on the counter for them to find tomorrow:

To Chanah Lindauer,

I have left with my husband Ascher Thanhausser. We are married since Thursday – under a chuppah – with ketubah and witness. I cannot marry David Ferd Soykher because I am already bamant, a married woman. It is done. Do not try to find me. Do not attempt to rescue me. The path of my life has changed and I go toward my destiny gladly and with abundant joy.

Marta Lindauer Thanhausser

The house has finally quieted. My heart pounds. Is it really time for me to leave this place? All right then. Zay gezunt… good-bye.

28 Av, 5549
August 20, 1789
Stuttgart

I waited even longer to make sure that everyone was sound asleep then I crept down those stairs silently avoiding the ones that creaked. I gathered some old fruit, three bagels and a half loaf of dark rye. There were onions piled on the counter so I took two of them. I grabbed a packet of salt, a small bag of beans and then I wrapped a hunk of kugel in a cloth and laid it in the top of my bag.

The last thing I was going to do before I left the note was fold one of the knives into a cloth so it would be safe to carry. Just as I was about to lay the knife down I heard the baby make a noise and when I looked up, Hindel was standing in the doorway to the room with Bertha on her hip. Her eyes turned into slits and I saw her haughtiness gather up.

'Well, well… what have we here?' She eyed my bags and my dress which was thickened with extra layers. I was caught!

When I tried to talk the only thing that came out was a squawk. Large dark flapping entities, like huge vultures, swirled through my vision. I'm certain I heard a cry from deep within my soul that sounded like a strangled goat.

I laid the knife down and tried to wrap it but my hands were shaking too much. The only thing I could think was that I needed to get out of there to meet Ascher.

Hindel slowly walked over to where I stood behind the counter.

'So where do you think you're going? Huh? And at this time of night?'

I knew I needed to stay calm but there were too many old feelings about her in me. The words spat themselves out:

'It's none of your business. Leave me alone.' I rolled the knife up and put it down the side of my bag then I tossed the note on the counter and turned to go.

Hindel scuttled around me until she blocked my way out the back door.

'Not so fast sister...' She had such a superior tone.

I knew it sounded stupid but in my panic the only thing I could think to say was, 'Leave me alone...'

I tried to push past her but she was not moving. And I didn't want to be too forceful because she had the baby in her arms. How I hated my sister just then. Why did she have to be in my way? Everything had been going so smoothly.

She looked again at the bags I carried then set her mouth. Her voice was icy.

'It looks like you're making a getaway! Are you

trying to jilt Ferd Soykher and run out on mother? Ha, you're really something Marta. You think you can just run away? Do whatever you want? Not a chance...' She shifted the baby around onto her other hip.

I had that storm going on inside me which made it nearly impossible to think or hear myself. I felt completely stupid and useless before her. Within moments I was the size of a raisin, with no idea what to do next. I remember the baby's eyes, they had a wide-open startled expression. She was fearful and so was I.

I turned to try to leave by the other door but when I did I saw my mother standing there disheveled and half-asleep. On a normal day she wakes up crabby and mean. You can imagine what she was like in the middle of the night. There was no escape for me.

'What's going on out here? Hindel, is the baby alright?'

'Oh yes Mother, she's just fine. It's Marta who's in trouble.'

All my feelings of ugliness and worthlessness came boiling up. Those two together knew how to make me feel small and hollow. They threw banter back and forth like cats toying with me, their prey.

And… I felt their jabs.

'She thinks she's queen of the world.'

'You little zoyne, you've never been any good…'

'Who do you think you are anyway?'

'You're going to steal food from your own family?'

'Ha this is a good one… Marta's running away!'

All said to make me feel like I was the stupidest person in the world. And I did feel stupid. Stupid and ashamed for even trying to imagine that I could just walk away from my horrible life.

'Guess what Missy, you're not going anywhere. You will marry David Ferd Soykher and I will finally be done with this wretched place." Said by my mother, of course.

I tried to hold on to my own reason for being there in the kitchen which was that I was on my way to go and be with Ascher, but I could feel my spirit sliding down into hiding, into that dark place.

Hindel walked over and handed the baby to our mother then grabbed one of my bags and started digging through it. Both of my booklets were in there along with my ink jar and quills. I saw what she was doing, I felt the horror of what she was doing but I couldn't move and I couldn't talk.

Hindel stood up with this very booklet in her hands. She was never a good reader but she peered in at the cover and read aloud:

'Listen to this: my diary, a small life, by Marta Lindauer, age 16 years 5 months... Ha ha... this ought to be good.'

Well something in me burst into flames. A gigantic boulder rolled its way up through me and, before I had a chance to think about it, erupted out of my mouth as a massive scream like I have never done before. It came out like vomit from a deeply buried fount. It kept coming and coming, wild and savage. All I could do was stand there and scream and scream and scream until my throat was raw.

I heard the children crying upstairs. Then there was a sharp knock at the back door which I answered before either Hindel or my mother could. It was Ascher. Turn around and I'm in a different life.

He took hold of my shoulders and looked into my face. 'Are you all right? I was waiting outside and heard you screaming.' He pulled me close and hugged me to him.

My mother blustered over toward us with her fists in the air: 'What, Gott im Himmel are you doing here? Get out of my inn at once, sir. You are not welcome here. What is going on?'

She stamped her foot – she looked evil.

Ascher squeezed in front of me and faced her. He kept me close with his arm around behind to hold my hand. I felt protected but I still wanted to disappear.

'Madam Lindauer...' he nodded once. 'I've come to take Marta away with me. She is my wife.' He stood tall. I was proud of him and proud to be his wife.

How do you think my mother reacted to this news? And Hindel, was she her usual kind sweet self? They both started shrieking at once... things like:

'You're lying!'

'You've no business stepping foot in this place.'

'Marta's getting married in a matter of hours...'

'Get away from her...'

And more of the same. My mother actually picked up a different knife from the counter and held it like a weapon, ready to slash my beloved. She was unhinged as I knew she would be.

Ascher didn't flinch. He looked right into my mother's eyes.

'Are you going to kill me, Madam Lindauer, because your daughter chose to marry me?'

She answered with a slimy callous voice. 'My daughter doesn't *choose* who she's going to marry. I signed a contract. We made a deal...'

'Pardon me Madam, but it's important that you understand. Marta and I are already married. Would you please put that knife back down on the counter?'

My mother lowered her hand but held on to the knife. Her mouth peeled back like a cur.

'If you try to take her away I'll slice you.'

I was breathless. My own mother threatened my own husband!

He gasped and then turned toward me. I could tell his patience was running out.

'Are you ready to take your leave?'

I couldn't believe we were going to walk out of there and leave them screeching behind us.

Then something happened.

The thumping in my chest faded away, my body stopped trembling, my hearing changed. I saw us in the room from a place outside of myself. My view was from above near the ceiling looking down. I saw how my mother and sister were behaving toward the girl in the scene, me. I didn't see Ascher but I felt him there close beside me. The vision didn't last long but after I saw it something fierce in me came to a sharp point.

'Be quiet!'

I had to say it three times because they were both acting crazy – yelling and throwing their arms around. My mother looked like the wrath of God. They were feeding off each other's indignation and self-righteousness.

So before I could think, loud words hurtled out of me toward them. I joined the fracas:

'I don't care what either of you think or say. I won't stay here in this house any longer. I'm leaving.'

The only way to describe it was: involuntary, like the scream that had ripped out of me earlier and brought Ascher in. I couldn't stop:

'You both make me sick with your superiority

and constant scorn. I'm an actual person, not just your slave. Did you really think I would marry that awful horse trader? I'm going to do what I want to do... and that is to go away with my husband Ascher Thanhausser.'

I can't remember exactly what I said but it was strong – maybe the strongest thing ever. My mother looked like she was shattering from the inside out. She was horrified that I was saying those things to her... like the universe was broken sideways. I guess for her it was.

I turned to Ascher.

'Now. Now I'm ready Ascher.'

He bent over and picked up one of the bags, the one with food in it, and I took the other. Then we turned to leave.

My mother was having a fit. She was acting like Hindel's two-year-old, stomping her foot, crying and moaning. They were both pathetic – I felt like the strong one. I wanted to be out of that place... away from the lunacy. As I closed the door behind us I said a few last things:

'Don't come looking for me... I'm never coming back. I never want to see either of you ever again.'

They were dumbfounded – rendered motionless,

so I left.

We gathered up Ascher's pack and my violin which he had left outside the door. I was shaking so hard and my throat was ragged. I had never acted like that in my entire life.

We walked as fast as we could up the Vorderer Judenberg. Neither of us said anything for a long time. There was little light so we hung on to each other and staggered up the hill until our distress turned into mirth.

When we realized that we were far enough away and alone together we hugged and danced and laughed hysterically and kissed and hugged some more. From a most awful scene to a most superb situation... all within an hour.

We walked and walked. Many times we had to jump behind some bushes when a horse and rider passed. Ascher didn't want anyone to know we were out there. Night sounds... owl, dove, insects, all kept us company.

One visit behind a dark hedgerow was our own precious time together... we were breathless. I didn't know that love could pour out from my heart for a man... but yes, it can.

The night air was mild and sweet. I ended up

leaving off an underskirt, a sweater and an extra blouse which made my bag heavier. But my darling husband took on more of the load and even though it was the middle of the night I felt light and free as a butterfly.

Once when we stood kissing, enraptured under the stars, my shoulders sprouted wings and I became a cherub – freshly hatched, ready to fly into my new life.

30 Av, 5549
August 22, 1789

When we got to the river Fils we turned west onto the road toward Stuttgart. We spent part of the first night in a forest near Uhingen and the second night on the floor of the main room in an inn in Esslingen, with others leaned up against the walls or curled up in a corner as we were. I can only say that the awful smells and vulgar snoring in that cramped place made it impossible to sleep.

I'm now writing this nearly last entry in my diary in Stuttgart. There's not much space left so I want to end this book with our journey away from Jebenhausen... Ascher's, mine and my beautiful violin's.

On our walk we had long conversations. When he asked me what I remembered about playing the violin I had to think for a long time about the answer.

I told him that my strongest memory was the sound of the violin. From the first time I heard it, it was familiar – like birds singing or insects buzzing. And better than anything I had ever heard before.

The first time I heard a violin was that night the musician came to the inn. Something deep inside me was struck by the rich beautiful melodies he played. Some kind of ancient spirit had been waiting there hoping to be rekindled and awakened in me. I just knew I had to learn to play that violin.

So I watched him closely to see how it was done and I decided to listen to Samuel's lessons so that someday I could make those beautiful haunting sounds, too.

Ascher told me that he loved hearing the music but it had never occurred to him to want to learn to play. He said that my desire and my ability were gifts from God.

Then in a kind way he asked me to tell him what happened with Samuel's violin teacher... my violin teacher. Voices inside me started screaming: don't tell him, don't remember that, leave it down in the locked place, don't don't don't...

But ever since I've been with Ascher as his wife I sometimes hear a reasonable voice, like a nice mother. And just then she said: 'You know that Ascher loves you. You know that he has never let you down. If your husband wants to know what happened to you when you were a girl it's alright to tell him.' Here's what I said:

'Ascher, it's not easy for me to talk about what happened... I'm getting shaky from thinking about it. I do want to tell you but I don't know how.' By then I could hardly talk... I could not come up with the right words.

All I could think was: I'm tired of swallowing down that horrid man's memory. And then the next thing I knew, I was heaving my lunch over the side of the road.

Afterwards I sat under a nearby tree and words started coming out. Then I couldn't stop myself. I told him what happened... what that man did to me, what he made me do. How he forced himself in every possible way into my body.

When I finally stopped talking, Ascher held me. His love felt steady and sure and true. I was so grateful for my mazl, my luck, to have Ascher by my side.

We walked for a while before I could talk again. He stayed quiet. When I looked at him I saw only love and concern for me in those eyes that I love more and more. So I kept talking.

'The violin teacher told me that if I did what he wanted and told no one then he would teach me to play as beautifully as he did. And you know that's what I wanted, to play like that more than anything... anything.'

'So the first time he showed me his... he made me... oh I can't say it. I can't! But he did hurt me and afterwards I was so ashamed. I felt so dirty. I ran up to my special place beside the pond... and there you found me.'

Tears rolled down Ascher's cheeks but I kept talking and told him more about the things that man did to me. I never wanted it... never! But I did want to learn to play the violin.

I told Ascher that even though I loved playing my violin more than anything, I felt ugly and bad all the time, even when I wasn't with that evil man. I felt equally as bad as a person as I felt good about playing music... both things at once and both things as far apart as two feelings could be.

After that conversation I was surprised at how easy it was to talk about other things with Ascher.

Ascher told me stories about his life before he came to Jebenhausen, about his own family, his students and his travels. Sometimes he made me laugh and when he talked about his parents and their love for each other and for their children, that made me cry. His family is so different from mine.

We talked about love. Love was not a word I ever heard in my home. It was not a subject that mattered.

Ascher said that he never thought he would find love like ours... he always assumed he would marry a woman the shadchan had chosen for him. He told me that his love for me is so strong, nothing will ever deter it.

I admit that we rolled around like children in the fragrant grass and had to jump up and assume a more respectable bearing when we heard a horse and wagon coming on the road. Once we resumed our walk we ventured into the subject of death.

I've never been afraid of dying the way some people are, like my mother. The thing I wonder about the most is: what does it feel like to die? I think it's a familiar feeling. Ascher said that remembering he will die reminds him that he's alive and how precious a gift it is that we're here at all. He said it makes him a better man.

I told Ascher that I do love him and that I want my love for him to grow. He said that it would because I want it to and because of how much he loves me. I never dreamed someone would love me the way he does. With his love I'm not a horrible person and my mind is more peaceful.

How strange it is to be out from under my mother's rule. I stepped sideways into a much better life... because of love. I didn't know this kind of thing could even happen.

It was glorious to be walking along roadsides and fields filled with sunshine and summer flowers. I had never taken a day away from the inn in my life.

But shadowy thoughts came over me often... I should be getting dinner ready or seeing to the guests. And then a bird would sing or Ascher would say something or the sunlight would flicker across my face and I would remember where I was. It made me giddy. I did not know that happiness could grow in me.

3 Elul, 5549
August 25, 1789

We've been in Stuttgart for six days and have taken a tiny room in the upstairs of the home of a generous widow named Tilde Hirsch. She has agreed to reduce our rent for some help around the house and for this we are grateful. We must put by every penny we can.

I am happy to assist her with the housekeeping, cooking and marketing. I don't mind because I need to have something useful to do while I wait for my violin to be repaired. Ascher has already made plans with the school to do some tutoring which he will take up first thing next week.

Stuttgart is a lively place. I've never seen so many people at once before. Everywhere I look there are merchants and peddlers, horses and mules, scholars, housewives and children bustling about, selling, buying, shouting greetings. The commotion is continuous and loud. Even though our room is small I'm relieved to return to it for some tranquility after being jostled about in the crowded streets.

The day after we arrived we set out with my broken violin in hand to find the luthier Lupot. Here I want to say that from the moment we discovered it in Heaven I have fully claimed this violin as my own. Its original owner is long gone and now it's mine... forever.

It wasn't easy to walk lady-like because I was

excited – I wanted to skip and dance along the streets. We had rough directions from Reb Veberke and made several wrong turns but did finally manage to locate the shop.

We were met at the door by the tall bony Lupot whose French accent was charming. And what a magical haven greeted us inside: a workbench strewn with tools and curled wood shavings and the sweet aroma of freshly carved wood and polish. Violins hung in rows from pegs on the wall which produced a frantic thump in my heart at the sight.

I barely breathed when we took my violin out of its wrap and showed it to the violinmaker. First he took up the back piece, peered in closely and read the label:

'Ah yes, Leopold Wilhelm of Nuremberg... I know of this maker... I have seen... several of his instruments. He does fine work... excellent work.' He nodded his approval. Bubbles of joy sprang up inside me.

Then he began his examination which took forever. He inspected every piece front and back, weighed its heft in his hands and pointed out details to us that I hadn't ever noticed before: the fineness of the inlaid wood all the way around the top which is called purfling, the delicacy and placement of the *f* -holes, the petite overall size which he attributed to its being a lady's violin and which makes my violin lighter to hold than most, the well-planed top, bottom and ribs and smooth shapely neck with inlaid fingerboard. And about the beautifully carved scroll, he said it resembles the work of some Italian violinmakers he's seen.

He admired the fine craftsmanship, the unusual yet balanced form with high arching and was impressed with the varnish. There was so much about violins that I didn't know before our visit to his shop.

After he finished his appraisal, Lupot crossed his arms and spoke in his slow way to Ascher:

'Sir... I... would like... to make you... an offer... for this... this fine instrument.'

I gasped and blurted out: 'Oh no sir, that can never happen. This is my violin and I haven't played it for seven years. Please just put it back together quickly so I can play it again!'

Although I was embarrassed by my own outburst I noticed that both men smiled.

Ascher reassured Lupot that I had meant what I said and added kindly that under no circumstances would we be interested in selling. He too wanted to know how long it would take for the repairs. The luthier had a slow careful manner. When he talked he took his time.

'Well... if I get on it right away.... I'm certain I can.... have it ready for you before.... three weeks are up.'

Three weeks! I didn't want to wait that long. He was obviously a man who did everything slowly.

'Is there any way we could get it sooner?' It popped out of my mouth before I thought and I was again embarrassed.

But Ascher in his kind way assured me that it wouldn't be a problem to wait. Then he gave Lupot the address where we're staying and then we had to leave my violin behind which wasn't easy for me. Will it ever really be put back together again?

When we left Ascher offered me his arm and escorted me down the street.

'Don't worry my darling, your violin is in good hands. And soon your precious friend will be where it belongs... with you. In the meantime we must be patient. I do, however, have an idea for us to think about...'

Then he told me his plan. He wants us to go to America... America! He said it's a good thing that the violin repairs will take so long because we'll need that much time to prepare for our journey. First we'll walk from here (Stuttgart) to Calais in France. And there we'll board a ship that will take us to America... unbelievable!

But, it will take us nearly a month to walk to Calais and there's fighting going on in France. Here in Stuttgart there are French soldiers and French sympathizers everywhere in the streets. It's too much... I don't want to think about any of it.

Before I blow out my candle I want to write about another thing that happened on our way home, after we left my violin with Lupot. We passed a small church on a side street and there, coming from opened shutters, we heard the most glorious sounds... of many violins... but not just violins.

There were low strings and middle tones, high violin voices and something so deep and resonant that my ribs vibrated from the sound.

In a moment I sputtered and lost my composure. I'd never heard such beautiful music before. All those instruments together: melodies and harmonies weaving around each other like laments and conversations, prayers and rejoicing... every human emotion, every nuance of nature, eternities delivered to us the listeners. It was magnificent!

The way the notes moved up and down and around reminded me of the Bach tunes that I used to play. The same runs, the same jumps from note to note. Hearing that music made my heart ache with longing. How I wanted just then to join in on my own violin and be a part of that superb sound.

Then I had that familiar fear again: would I even be able to play my violin at all? What if my ability to play was blotted out by my black memories of that awful man? What if I sounded terrible when I tried to play it?

A bad feeling returned in my stomach. And in an instant the color went out of the world and my thoughts went down fast. Some moments went by when I couldn't even hear the music. I was so lost in my own dark thoughts which sounded like a loud wind in my ears, telling myself how awful and stupid I was.

Ascher must have noticed I was in distress. He put his arm around my shoulder and spoke softly in my ear. I stood up straighter and then the music broke through. After a few minutes I was restored and we listened together until the end of the piece.

After the music stopped we watched several people leave the church carrying their instruments. As an older woman with a violin case under her arm passed by, I couldn't help myself...

'Madam, that was the most beautiful thing I have ever heard. Thank you so much.' When she stopped and smiled at me I added: 'I hope to be able to play like that some day.'

'Oh,' she blinked at me. 'Do you play the violin?'

'Well, I played when I was small and now my own violin is being repaired at Lupot's shop...'

She interrupted. 'Lupot... yes... good. He's a reputable maker. He'll do a fine job.'

Ribbons of thrill streamed through me. 'I haven't played since I was nine. I don't know if I'll even be able to do it again.'

She looked closely into my eyes. I couldn't believe what she said next. 'Would you like for me to give you a lesson?'

This woman didn't know me or anything about me. Yet she offered to teach me! I turned to Ascher and saw that he had a reserved look on his face for the reason that we both knew well... we have no extra money. He couldn't give approval so I turned to the woman with a little smile, holding back my true feelings.

'Thank you, ma'am. My name is Marta

Lindauer... I mean Marta Thanhausser, and this is my husband Ascher Thanhausser. We're staying with the widow Hirsch in the Jewish section.' I wanted to let her know right away that we're Jewish so there wouldn't be any misunderstandings about that. But the information didn't appear to bother her at all.

She nodded. 'Glad to meet you both. My name is Anneliese Braun. I teach several children how to play the violin and I would be happy to help you, Marta.'

I was grateful but I knew we couldn't afford to pay her. A sinking feeling dropped through me. 'Madam Braun, I can't thank you enough for this offer...'

I could barely get the words out: A chance to learn more about how to play the violin? And right there before me? I used great control to keep from crying.

'...But we are not in a position to hire a teacher. It's something I would very much like to do but I'm afraid we can't right now.'

I had to turn aside because tears did arrive and I was ashamed. I wanted to walk away but I pulled myself together and faced the woman again. She had a kind face and held herself upright with natural confidence. I wondered if I would ever feel that kind of self-assurance.

She had been watching me and looked me right in the eye as she made up her mind:

'Marta, I would like to get together with you anyway. It doesn't matter whether you pay me or not. You appear to be a highly sensitive young woman with a love for the violin. For me, that's enough. I'll try to come up with some way for you to repay me that doesn't require money, all right? And you can use one of my violins at the lesson. How does that sound to you?'

Well, I jumped up and down right there on the street. First I hugged Ascher and then I bowed to Madam Braun. More tears, though this time of happiness, and we made arrangements for a violin lesson tomorrow at her home.

She lives several blocks from Tilde Hirsch but it will only take me a few minutes to get there. Oh happiness! Oh joy! Tomorrow I shall play a violin again. I can't believe it... I can't wait.

In that moment as now, my heart was full of gratitude.

I made a promise to myself to keep trying to stay in the bright real world with Ascher instead of *always pitching downward inside toward loathing when something reminds me of my old life. I may not always succeed but in this case, always trying is what matters most.*

My Diary

A NEW LIFE

by

Marta Lindauer Thanhausser

Stuttgart, Germany

10 Elul, 5549

September 1, 1789

This is the beginning of my second book. It has been nearly a week since I've written anything because two terrible things happened. Ascher and I had our first disagreement and now he lies pale and still in the bed beside me... severely ill.

He has a fever that has raged for four days and he's too weak to get out of bed. He suffers from constant terrible headaches and his throat is raw to the point that he can swallow almost nothing, not even light broth.

I have no words to describe my fear. This town is overcome with influenza. Each morning the undertakers cart off corpses of those poor souls who have not survived the night. It's an appalling sight that upsets every morsel of me.

I'm certain that I caused this terrible sickness to take hold in Ascher. If I hadn't upset him so Ascher wouldn't have gotten sick.

I came home from my violin lesson with Madam Braun acting like queen of the world. When Ascher asked me about it I strutted and boasted and repeated the things she had said to me: that I have an immense talent, that I should consider serious violin study, that I shouldn't leave Germany yet, that I should become more proficient on the violin and other such flattering things.

Ascher's face dropped. he lowered his voice. 'Is this what you really want to do, Marta? Stay here in Germany?'

And like a fool I didn't hesitate.

'Yes... oh yes Ascher. It's what I've wanted for so long... to play my violin and play it well. And now that I've heard a string orchestra I want to learn to do that too here in Stuttgart with all those other players and Madam Braun as my teacher...'

Ascher was still. He spoke with a low quiet voice:

'Well Marta, let me understand... what you're saying is that our trip to America is not as important to you as is staying here in Stuttgart and becoming an accomplished violinist?'

I failed to read the feelings behind his words, I had thoughts only for myself.

'Yes Ascher. That's right. I want to stay here and study with Madam Braun. I don't want to go to America.'

I watched Ascher's mouth draw down. He cleared his throat a few times and held his hand gently around his neck as though he was trying to keep warm. Now I know why he did that but at the time I didn't understand. There was something bothering him – I had never seen him like that.

'The plan that we made together was to walk to Calais and take a boat to America where you'll certainly be able to find someone to give you violin lessons, Marta. Why do you need to stay here to do that?'

I was too embarrassed to tell him that I was afraid to make the voyage. Here's what I said:

'Madam Braun told me that a cousin of hers made the crossing and wrote to her afterward that it was a horrible experience. Why don't we stay here, Ascher? That way I can become a real violinist and you can teach at the school.'

He looked down for a long time and when he finally looked up at me his eyes were rimmed with redness and his voice was raspy.

'As Jews, there is nothing for us here in Europe, Marta... nothing. But, there are abundant opportunities awaiting us in the New World. Now that we have left the protections of Jebenhausen our best prospects are in America. I want this for us, Marta... for us... for our children, God willing.'

At that moment I was the worst kind of wife. I crossed my arms with a big harrumph and then realized in the next moment that I was a fool.

I had been feeling wildly free thinking only of my

own future, my own desires. But that isn't something a woman or a wife can do for long. When I remembered that Ascher needed me by his side I was ashamed of my own behavior.

I begged his forgiveness and told him that I will go wherever he chooses regardless of my fears. And I meant it.

He barely lifted a hand to brush my arm and I thought that he was still not happy with me. When he trudged slowly up the stairs without looking back I was sure we would never be close again the way we had been since we left Jebenhausen. But Ascher was falling ill and I didn't know it.

11 Elul, 5549
September 2, 1789

What will happen now? Will my sweet husband survive? And even if he does, how will he ever be strong enough to walk to Calais? We need to leave by the middle of September if we're to make the ocean crossing before winter.

And what about the extra money he was going to earn tutoring at the Jewish school? That money was going to help pay for our passage overseas. Otherwise, when we get there, someone will own us for seven years.

Tilde Hirsch and I have tried every remedy we can think of but Ascher is so sick. She has sent for the barber and the rabbi.

Later... The barber had us make a poultice of garlic and onions and we also steeped some garlic broth with dozens of cloves mashed into the liquid. We're forcing willow tea down Ascher's throat whenever he's awake, too. The barber said it's rare but he has seen people survive the influenza with such measures. He said it is God's will and God's will alone who should live and who should die.

After many applications of the poultice and gallons of tea Ascher's heavy cough has subsided the smallest bit. Tilde and I see this as a good sign.

He's sleeping in the bed next to where I'm seated at the little table in our room. The rabbi hasn't come yet. He's busy visiting the families of those who haven't survived, God forbid.

12 Elul, 5549
September 3, 1789

In one week my violin will be repaired and after that we are supposed to leave on our voyage to

America. Gott im Himmel, what will happen?

I've grown fond of Tilde Hirsch our landlady. She's the reason I'm writing now in the middle of the afternoon. She always asks me questions about myself: What I used to do with my time when I still lived in Jebenhausen and what my family was like. That's a subject I have plenty of words for.

I ask her questions back – we're getting to know each other. She told me that at thirteen she was married off to a man who turned out to be wicked and whose mistreatment she endured for thirty-four years (which she described but which was too personal and awful to write down). He died five years ago.

She said that this part of her life, the part after being married, has felt like a gift. She said she's learning how to enjoy life... maybe for the first time.

Although I worry that my happiness with Ascher will remind her of what she never had, she assures me that isn't the case. Today after our midday meal when I was peeling beets she came up and put her arm around me. I hadn't even noticed that I was crying but when she touched me like that I set my knife down and sobbed into her shoulder.

When I could finally talk I told her the things I'd been worrying about: Ascher's still so sick, what if he dies, then what will I do? He's all I have... I can't live without him!

Tilde sat with me at the table and after I stopped bawling she told me a couple of things. The first was, 'Think about this, Marta... his illness is not getting worse.'

When she said that I realized she was right. That alone calmed a fearful vibration that had started up in me and remained active since the moment I realized he was sick.

Then she said, and with the utmost kindness and sympathy, 'He may die, Marta, but – God forbid you should have to – you *can* live without him...'

She was about to say something else but I interrupted her.

'No! You don't understand. Ascher is the only person in the world who... who loves me and cares about me. He knows who I am and he still loves me.'

Tilde had such concern folded into her face. I couldn't help it, I cried again. When I had collected myself she talked to me.

'But, Marta... you are loveable. Why, I love you and I've only known you for two weeks.' She made me smile. 'And, I can't wait to hear your violin.

You'll play for me won't you?'

I knew I should have felt happy to hear her say that but I just blubbered some more. I couldn't control my tears so we both let them continue until they wore themselves out.

I apologized but she said it's good to get that sadness out of me and I did feel better afterwards. Still, Ascher was in the bed upstairs. How good could I feel?

She took ahold of my hand and rubbed her thumb across my index finger over an ink stain smudged on the knuckle.

'What's this mark from, Marta? Have you been writing with quill and ink?'

I decided it would be alright for her to know that I keep a diary so I told her that I have filled one booklet and started the second. When I mentioned that I have already written the entire story of my life since I first met up with Ascher again, after Samuel died, she became solemn and looked right into my eyes.

'You must take time to write, Marta. Your gifts are God-given – you must use them.' She was serious.

'Sheynkeyt,' (her pet name for me which means

beauty) 'I want you should go upstairs – spend the rest of the afternoon – write in your book. You must write about Stuttgart, and being a beloved bride, and how beautiful is the garden in this afternoon light...'

She insisted, I was surprised. I have only ever done my writing in secret when I'm done with my days' work or in the early morning before I've begun. I hugged her, ran up to our room and here I am now writing in my new book. I have had several hours of time to myself to do it. Incredible!

18 Elul, 5549
September 9, 1789

This afternoon we received word from a messenger that my violin is ready. However, Ascher is not. He's so weak he can barely lift a hand or even sit up on his own. He's thin as an insect and his skin is still pale and gray. All he wants to do is sleep and Tilde assures me that's what he should do. Oh but my happiness is a fount of sparkling light – Ascher is going to live... I think... I hope.

I'm dying to collect my violin but Ascher isn't strong enough to make the visit to Lupot's with me yet and I don't want to go without him. For now his rest is the most important thing.

I had to retreat to the garden after breakfast. I knew I was horrid because I couldn't stop thinking about my violin or feeling the craving for it – the desire, the desperate need. I knew I shouldn't be impatient. I should think about Ascher and getting him well. But my heart told me something else, that very soon I would hold my precious violin and play the melodies I remember from when I was little.

Then the dark voices came: 'You don't even think about the right things. You're stupid. You can't do anything right. What makes you think you deserve love? You're an imbecile – ugly and worthless. You deserve to die...'

Why did I feel so awful about wanting to play the violin? What's so wrong with wanting both Ascher and my violin? I asked Tilde this question after our mid-day meal and also described those dark voices to her.

'Why do you tell yourself that you're bad, Marta?'

What a direct question. I hadn't ever considered why I do that even though I know I am... bad.

So I told her: 'Well my mother always told me

that I was bad. Everything I ever did was wrong. I was born wrong. I'm flawed. I know this.'

Tilde looked at me with curiosity. 'You seem like a well-put-together young woman to me. You have chosen well in Ascher, you have left a situation that was harmful to you, to your spirit, and you are forging ahead with a new life. You can be proud of yourself, Marta. I encourage you to try to stop repeating those hurtful things in your head that were said to you long ago. That only makes you feel bad.'

I understood: 'I know. I wish I could.'

She folded a napkin and creased the edge with her fingernail. "Practice loving yourself rather than berating your own existence.'

I had never thought of that.

'Also, there is nothing wrong with loving Ascher and wanting your violin back, too. Both things are alright for you to be feeling. We humans, we have lots of feelings… it's part of being alive. The best thing you can do is to try to be kind to yourself Marta no matter what you are feeling.'

It was good to hear her say those things but I'm not sure that I can love the entire mixed up person who is me. Some days I can, some days I can't.

She kept talking. 'You are the one who changed your life, Marta... not Ascher. You made the choices for yourself that led you away from Jebenhausen to a better life. You are precious, a gifted child of God, and you are about to have some happiness in life. Don't listen to inner voices that tell you otherwise... they're plain wrong.'

We both smiled. I mostly believe she's right... I should be over those dark thoughts. After all, I have a wonderful husband who loves me and a new life, away from my past.

But it's not so easy to leave it all behind when those memories seem to have traveled with me in great trunks of storage within.

'Keep your sights on the future, Marta. Don't allow the past to haunt you or make you feel wrong or bad because you're neither one!'

Well she doesn't know what I really did when I was nine. She doesn't know how wretched I feel when I remember all that happened. I am damned forever for being that shameless little girl. My desire to learn to play the violin was so strong, so powerful that I went along...

She put her hand over mine and looked right into my eyes. 'It doesn't matter what happened back then. All that matters now is for us to nurture

Ascher back to health so that you two can collect your violin and set off on your journey.'

I'm not used to being around people who care about me and treat me so kindly. My first reaction was to mistrust her open displays of affection and concern. But she was genuine. Deep down I knew this was how it should be – this was how people were supposed to treat each other.

All I know is: I love Tilde Hirsch and love has strong power. Before Ascher and Tilde, except for Samuel, I have never felt the effects of love so strongly. Its sturdy arms hold me up. Love feels like medicine. It flows into wounds that were desperate to feel better – it soothes away shaky fears. It must take a long time before all the awful remembering goes away. Does it ever?

21 Elul, 5549
September 12, 1789
Saturday night

Ascher Thanhausser is my true love... and he will live! He told me this afternoon as we sat during Shabbos that it was not only the things Tilde and I did to help him get better that made him well. He insisted that our deep love was the real reason.

He said that all he could think about when he was sick was hearing me play my violin again. The memory of those sounds pulled him toward healing and gave him the strength to fight against death.

'But it was you, my love,' he told me, 'that I could not leave behind.'

We're certain that we are bashert – ordained to be together by our great universe. I'm wrapped in a cloak of gratitude. Ascher is my partner and my strength. He's steady and true. He is my gift.

More good news: We will see my violin in two days! Those little Bach tunes have been coming back to me. I'm constantly humming. It helps conquer anxious thoughts and it's a way to practice my violin in my mind.

In my mind I've been bowing and fingering everything I can remember over and over. I feel the violin on my shoulder under my chin, its neck in my hand, my fingers on the fingerboard, the bow pulling against the edges of the strings. The excellent union of earthly movements and magical response that brings forth beauty from another realm.

Yesterday, I took a long slow walk with Ascher who is better daily. We went out of the town and up a path along a high ridge that overlooks

Stuttgart and the lands beyond. We're planning to walk every day to get ready for our trip to Calais. His strength grows and my thankfulness along with it.

He pointed out the route across the valley that we're going to take when we leave early on Wednesday, four days from now. He's excited and so am I but I'm also scared... my poor stomach.

We do have some good luck because Ascher can speak French. He's been studying English too and has been teaching me a few words. I can say good day and thank you.

I'm going to carry a rucksack, a bag in each hand and my violin. Ascher said we'll find food for each day in the villages along the way to Calais so what we need to carry is what we'll take with us on the ship.

Tilde and I have been baking hard biscuits and drying apples, pears, sliced carrots and some other fruits and vegetables that will keep as dried. Two months is a long time. We'll both be thin as broom straw when we get to America – if we get there. I can't bear to imagine what Ascher will look like. He already resembles a walking stick.

Now I must return to the kitchen to help my friend with supper. I'll write more after the momentous occasion occurs of retrieving my violin from Lupot and trying to play it again after seven years.

The next two days will take a month. I'm certain that I'm going to be struck dead tonight. A dread disease will throw me to bed tomorrow. When I imagine holding that delicate put-back-together violin I crumple to bits inside.

24 Elul, 5549
September 15, 1789

This might be my last entry while I live in Germany because in four days we'll walk across the border into France. I plan to stow my ink and quills deep inside my pack so they'll survive. If I can I'll write along the way but I think it might be better to wait until I unpack – on the boat maybe.

Last night was not my best night. I was awake so much that I finally got up, went downstairs and walked through to the garden behind the house. There was a sliver of moon and stars as thick as the spots on an old speckled roan. When I saw those pinpoints of light I thought of eternity, that long everlasting truth. I thought of my small self – so important to me, so insignificant in the universe.

I listened to the night sounds: frogs, bird chirps and the wind blowing through the leaves. Being alive is a gift. I want to be worthy of my time here. I want to be a good wife and... I want to play my violin again!

Fear is always with me yet my new life opens before me with happiness and even joy. I wake up excited every morning.

Sometimes I do get caught by ugly voices inside that want to take me over and then I'm suddenly ten years old with no way to cope... dragging Hindel's nastiness along with me everywhere I go.

Life outside of me and life inside of me did not agree back then. I moved through my days and nights clutching at my throat for deliverance from the human mistake that was my self. I was not innocent of anything, not even of being born. I was wrong for being born.

I only knew that I, Marta Lindauer, was the very schism that my being in the world seemed to produce. My face felt jagged, ugly and uneven. That's how I saw myself. It was a permanent hell with no escape possible... ever.

I wonder what got me through all those years. Was it the distant memory of my brother's love? For so long I lived in darkness.

Now when I wake up next to my husband, a good kind man, I know how lucky I am. I'm in a different life. Ascher praises me for my bravery and strength. He says I'm his hero. I say a soul must have its way. I only did what I had to do.

I heard small skittering animals in the grasses around me. I went back to bed after that and slept until Ascher roused me.

'Marta, your day has arrived. Wake up, my dove. Today is the day!'

I pulled him on top of me and covered him with kisses. When he looked into my eyes I resolved to stay in a good mood all day. Nothing was going to ruin one of the most important days of my life.

I was a determined coach horse pulling at the bit all the way to Lupot's shop. The tinkling bell, the scents of wood and varnish, all those violins hung in a row... every bit of it welcomed me back and so did Lupot. He had my violin lying on velvet on the counter, put back together and gleaming.

I rushed over and picked it up but when I did a memory came unbidden to me. That man's smell... his face... his hands. It was as though Samuel's violin teacher was standing right beside me. I set the violin down and stumbled backwards. I think I cried out.

Ascher took me in his arms and held me. Some time passed before I could even open my eyes. When I did I found myself still in Lupot's shop with the Luthier calmly waiting and no sign of that man. How real that visitation had seemed. But I wasn't going to let his memory ruin this day.

I gathered up my courage and tried again. This time I took a few moments to look again at my beautiful violin. There was no sign of brokenness. It was perfect, the same as I remembered only a bit darker.

Yes I had tears but they were tears of happiness. When I felt I couldn't wait another second I lifted it and held it close like I used to do. How can I describe that moment? Could a mother retrieving her long-lost child be any happier than I felt then?

My thumb strummed the strings – a sound I had waited seven years to hear. My heart thumped hard and fast. Neither man said a word. I found the newly re-haired bow on the counter and picked it up in my right hand. I put the violin on my left shoulder and rested my chin on it.

My arm shook but I placed the bow on the D string and pulled my first note. It sounded deep and rich and wonderful! A thrill started in my feet and shivered its way up through my shoulders and out the top of my head.

My initial notes were hesitant but it took only a few down bows and up bows before my arms and fingers took off on their own. A Bach dance poured out of me through the violin and the voice I heard in the music was familiar. It was a sound I remembered – the mirror of my very own soul.

I was filled with joy, moving the bow and fingers and bringing forth delight into the silence of the room. Behind those notes, surrounding the music was that feeling of lightness and peace I recalled from when I was nine.

My arms were happy. My fingers danced. I closed my eyes and played and played, so happy to hear those precious and cherished sounds again.

How long I played I do not know. Finally when I couldn't remember any more I stopped. When I opened my eyes I found I had moved around until I was facing away from Ascher and Lupot!

It was the first time ever I had played music that wasn't forbidden. I sent a prayer of thanks to the heavens. I knew just then that I was the luckiest girl in the world and no matter what happened after that my life's dream had already been fulfilled. I hugged my violin and thanked Ascher and Lupot for bringing us back together.

When I looked into Ascher's eyes they were brimming with tears.

'That sounded glorious, my darling. Shall we head back to Madam Hirsch's?'

He turned to Lupot. 'We leave early tomorrow morning for America! Thank you for your fine work...' and so on. I can hardly remember any of it – I was in a frenzy of elation.

Lupot looked at the violin in my arms. 'I have heard... from some associates... that Leopold Wilhelm, the maker of this violin, has passed away.'

There was a long pause before he spoke again. 'Considering... the quality of the craftsmanship in this instrument... I would say that you own a rare and valuable violin. I don't know... how many he made... while he was alive... but this one is exquisite.'

To me, my violin has a value above any amount of money. Ascher paid the Luthier and then we packed up the violin and bow and walked back to Madam Hirsch's home, or I should say... I floated above the ground all the way there!

We're completely packed and ready to leave early tomorrow. Ascher has recovered enough that he says he will be fine as long as he is able to pause for rest along the way. When I look at him it's hard to believe that he'll have the strength to do it. But there's no more to say – we must leave now in order to arrive in Calais in time for the final embarkation of the season. As it is, sailing this late in the year will make our trip even more fraught with danger from the changing seasons so we must go now.

The only problem is we don't have enough money. Our purse would be adequate if Ascher had worked for these past three weeks at the school instead of testing death. Whenever we talk about this Ascher's mouth tightens, he squints his eyes as though looking off into a frightening future and shakes his head. Then he hunches his shoulders and tells me not to worry, God will provide. I hope so.

This evening turned out to be a much grander send-off than either of us were expecting. Tilde and I worked all day in order to store as many provisions as we could in our bags. My violin waited impatiently on the shelf but I couldn't get to it because of my tasks.

Finally when we had finished our work Tilde and I made some supper and sat down with Ascher to our last meal with her in Stuttgart. There was little conversation – we're all tired and nervous about the whole thing.

I did have enough left in me after our meal to

take out my violin and play a few tunes. While I was playing the rabbi stopped by to wish us well then excused himself. He was so taken with the melodies that he left and returned a few minutes later with several others from town, including Madam Braun.

They all sat around Tilde's parlor and clapped and stomped their feet in time to the music. A lively and cheerful feeling enveloped us all. I felt free as a bird – closed my eyes and played with a depth and richness I had never heard before until I couldn't play another note.

Loud clapping surrounded me, the first I had ever received in my life. It sprang up the moment I stopped and what a gratifying sound. I couldn't believe it was all for me. I was just doing what I love to do.

I hadn't noticed how many people from town had crowded into the room but there might have been twenty or more. Some were folks I had gotten to know during our stay with Tilde.

Then a wonderful thing happened. One of the men, the tailor, reached into his pocket, pulled out a coin and set it in the middle of the table. Another did the same. Within a few moments every person in that room had placed a coin or two on the table.

The rabbi stood and spoke: 'We're grateful to hear such beautiful music, Madam Thanhausser.'

He bowed toward me then stood up straight and continued: 'We pray you and your husband will be safe on your journey and will make your way to the New World as excellent representatives of the Jewish people here in Germany. We know your musical gifts will help pave the way. And, you have such a fine instrument to carry with you, too. May God make his light to shine upon you...'

He made a benediction over us all and we were blessed.

Ascher's eyes spilled over and mine did too. What generosity... what kindness... we were overcome with gratitude. There were heartfelt thanks all around and then the evening was ended.

Before I climbed Tilde's stairs for the last time she and I embraced. I thanked her the best I could but my heart was full and my voice faltered. Then she slid her lovely blue shawl off her own shoulders, wrapped it around mine and said:

'To me you are special. Wear this shawl in good health, and always remember to be kind to yourself. I will never forget you, Marta. Good luck.'

What an end to a miraculous day.

My beloved husband sleeps beside me. At dawn we set off for France, away from everything we have ever known.

Our packs sit piled in the corner. Resting on top is my very own violin... which I hope to play some day soon... in America, our new home.

Acknowledgements

Writing this book has been a monumental undertaking. My hope was to create a compelling story with authentic characters who could bring illumination into the dark world of abuse that so many children must endure. I am grateful to all of those who have provided assistance in my endeavor to foster greater understanding and help promote healing.

Fortunately, I have been together with Paul Umbarger since 2001. The balance we have been able to achieve as artists, spouses, creative partners, co-parents and soul mates is a delicate and wonderful thing. Paul's belief in me, his patience, generosity, love and excellent skills on Word and Photoshop, along with his astute editing prowess, are the reasons that my manuscript became a book. Thank you, Paul, with all my heart. We are lucky beyond compare.

In May 2017, we visited Germany to do research in Nuremberg and Jebenhausen. While in Jebenhausen we were most fortunate to spend time with Dr. Karl-Heinz Reuss, who helped create the first Jewish museum in Germany, in Jebenhausen, in 1992. He guided us through the museum and shared his considerable knowledge so that we more fully understood the history of the Jewish people there from 1777 to 1942. Then, he took us to the home that had belonged to my family, where my great-grandmother was born, and also to the old Jewish cemetery where we found the graves of four of my direct ancestors. I am immeasurably grateful to Dr. Reuss, not only for his personal hospitality, but also for his dedication to documenting and memorializing the lives of the Jewish people of Württemberg.

Some of the best practical information from any source came from my oldest son, Joe Price. When I wanted to know, for instance, what would have been on the kitchen counter in the Lindauer inn, or even how an inn was set-up and run in 1782, I needed only to ask Joe and before long I would receive a wealth of articulate, accurate and personalized information. For all his generous and loving assistance, I give my utmost thanks and appreciation.

Thank you to my sister, Ruth Reid, for her constant love and support. In those harrowing moments when my confidence faltered, her steadfast encouragement held me up.

My father-in-law, Lloyd Umbarger, provided consistency, support and reassurance throughout the entire process of writing this book. He and my mother-in-law, Sara, listened to early drafts and gave me essential encouragement to keep going. I offer grateful thanks to Lloyd and Sara, for their generosity has been invaluable and life sustaining.

Thank you also, to our other wonderful and supportive sons: Charley Umbarger, Jake Duscha and Louis Umbarger for helping to create a family that I am super proud of.

Knowing and working with Maureen Higgins has been a most important gift in my life. I thank her for helping me live and for believing in this story, and me, from the very beginning.

I am also grateful to friends, family members and others who, among other things, served as readers, critics and faithful cheerleaders during the book's gestation. Special thanks to: Dr. SooJin Pate, Ingrid Liepins, Laura Lynn, Jayne Moon, Joanne Weiner, Muriel Levy, Lily Gillespie, Anneliese Weiss, Mary Corddry, Dr. Sandra Murphree, Marianne McNee, Holley Humphrey, Jim Umbarger, Bill McNee, Andrew Dipper, Ludger Geiger and Dr. Stefan Rohrbacher.

About the Author

Caren Simon Umbarger has played the violin since the age of five. She earned a BA in violin performance from Hamline University and has been a professional musician, conductor and string teacher for more than 35 years. Her first novel, *Coming To: A Midwestern Tale,* won a 2011 Florida Book Award bronze medal for General Fiction.

Caren is the owner of a beautiful old violin, made in Nuremberg in 1782 by Leopold Widhalm, that wound up being the inspiration for this story. In 2011, moments before shipping it off to be sold, Caren reconsidered. Rather than parting with her old friend, she was compelled, instead, to write a book about it. The result, six years in the making, is her second novel, *The Passion of Marta.* Widhalm's violin graces both the front and back covers of the book.

The author's family heritage played a significant role in the confluence of ideas that brought forth Marta's story. Caren's maternal great-grandmother, Rosa Rohrbacher Schlesinger, was born in Jebenhausen and emigrated to America at the age of 16. Her paternal grandfather, Dr. Frank Simon, was a renowned American band director and teacher, who enjoyed a long and celebrated career which included seven years as the principal cornet soloist and assistant conductor for John Phillip Sousa.

Caren Umbarger is confident that Wilhelm's lady's violin holds more secrets and has further tales to tell. She and her husband live, work & play in St. Augustine Beach, Florida.